Praise for L.C. Monroe's *Meagan's Chance*

5 Angels and Recommended Read! "Great job to L.C. Monroe for her imaginative mind and for bringing romance with God to make a tale that will enchant you until the end."

~ Lena C., Fallen Angel Reviews

5 Blue Ribbons "This touching and deeply moving story is so much more than just a romance between a man and a woman; it's more than just a book that centers on faith and belief, it's a journey and in the end a family is born. MEAGAN'S CHANCE is beautifully written and is one of the best books I've read all year."

~ *Lina C., Blue Ribbon Reviews*

3.5 Klovers! "The emotion and belief in God's Master plan is surely palatable and was brought home in an emotional and non-preachy way that is simply lovely and heartwarming. For me, Ms. Monroe is a master story-teller in whatever genre she chooses and Meagan's Chance is proof that she can make you sigh in appreciation of whatever genre she puts her mind to."

~ Marilyn Rondeau, (RIO), CK2's Kwips and Kritiques

Meagan's Chance

L.C. Monroe

A SAMHAIN PUBLISHING, LTD. publication.

Samhain Publishing, Ltd.
577 Mulberry Street, Suite 1520
Macon, GA 31201
www.samhainpublishing.com

Meagan's Chance
Copyright © 2008 by L.C. Monroe
Print ISBN: 978-1-59998-791-0
Digital ISBN: 1-59998-475-X

Editing by Angela James
Cover by Scott Carpenter

First Samhain Publishing, Ltd. electronic publication: July 2007
First Samhain Publishing, Ltd. print publication: May 2008

Chapter One

"Old German-Town Road? He didn't say anything about an Old German-Town Road," Meagan O'Hare muttered to herself as she tried to read the map spread out on the passenger seat of her car.

She narrowly avoided collision with a dusty pickup slowing for a turn in front of her. Hay flew loosely around her car and she sneezed. Darn allergies. She reluctantly turned down the fan on her car's air conditioner. Patty told her that Oregonians rarely saw the sun, much less felt its heat. So where had this ninety-degree-plus day come from?

Meagan had the distinct feeling that she was nowhere near her friend's home. One minute she had been traveling through downtown Portland and the next she found herself in the middle of farm country. Certain she had followed Jake's directions to the letter, Meagan glared at the expanse of farmland out her window. Patty had definitely told her that they lived in subdivision. This would be the last time she took directions from Patty's husband. He could probably draw her a map of ancient Israel from memory, but was hopeless when it came to anything more recent.

The thought did not make her smile. Meagan's patience was about used up.

She was hungry.

She was cranky.

Pretty soon she would be out of gas.

Groaning, she tried to ignore the blinking light on her dashboard that was her car's Morse Code for "low on fuel".

Blaring lyrics from Petula Clark's "Downtown" on the local oldies station weren't helping either. She'd give her new lime green tennis shoes to see a street sign right now, much less any downtown. Leaning over, she flipped off the radio.

Lord, please help me. You know I'm lost and I need a gas station. Soon.

Words tumbled through her stressed-out brain. *Trust in the Lord with all your heart and lean not on your own understanding.*

Okay, okay, I trust you! But, please help me!

Ahead, Meagan noticed a driveway entrance. Praise God. It was the first one she'd seen in over a mile. *Thank you, Lord, thank you.* Her thanks turned to disbelief when her car started to shimmy. Meagan's teeth rattled as the Escort shuddered to a halt. Getting out of the vehicle, Meagan knew what she would find.

The tire looked like it had exploded. Kicking it did nothing to allay her frustration.

Looking up at the sky, she said, "I wasn't even speeding."

Meagan trudged around the automobile to find her jack and tire iron. Kneeling next to the car, Meagan lifted the lug wrench and tried to place it over a bolt. She turned it one way and then another, but it wouldn't take grip. Struggling with each bolt, Meagan finally had to admit defeat.

Her tire iron was the wrong size.

This day had just gone from bad to worse. First, that editor at the writers' conference had told her not to bother sending her manuscript in. They weren't buying fantasy children's books right now. Then she had gotten lost and almost run out of gas on the way to Patty and Jake's.

Shoot and now this. Her tire was blown and she had no way to change it. At least she was near a house. That was something. Considering the lack of houses along this road, it was actually almost a miracle.

Okay, okay. Thanks.

Locking her car, she turned and walked up the long drive to a Victorian-style farmhouse. The wrap-around porch looked inviting and Meagan wished she could just collapse on one of the wicker chairs.

She rang the doorbell. What she needed was a telephone and a tow truck. Or a tire iron that fit, she thought ruefully. She started in surprise when the door flew open almost before she had taken her finger from the doorbell. Even more startling was the fact that no one stood on the other side.

In the recess of the hall Meagan could see an older woman wearing a housekeeping uniform waving her arms frantically. Her distress was at odds with the calm gentility of the house. Sun glinted through shining windows onto a hall table graced with a vase of summer blooms.

"Excuse me, but is everything all right?" It would be in keeping with this day to find herself in the middle of a domestic crisis.

The housekeeper didn't answer her question, but turned to wave Meagan inside. She called down the hall. "Jason *y* Mandicita. *Vente me.*"

Meagan waited until the woman turned back toward her to speak. "Hello, my name is Meagan O'Hare. I got lost and—"

Meagan got no farther before two children came sailing down the stairs toward her. Her heart accelerated in fear that one or both of them would trip and fly headfirst down the steep stairway. They stopped inches away and stood gawking at Meagan as if she were a sideshow at the circus. She stared back.

Meagan's heart constricted with familiar longing. She knew that she had to get over this preoccupation with children, but how? Her marriage might be over, but the desire to become a mother that had driven her the past five years had not dissolved along with it.

A blond boy who looked about nine or ten scuffed his tennis shoe against the hardwood floor while he measured her with a look. "Cool."

Cool? What was that supposed to mean?

"She looks nice." Twisting a brown curl around her finger, the small girl smiled shyly at Meagan while she spoke.

Meagan opened her mouth and nothing came out. She looked nice? If she didn't use the phone and leave pretty soon they'd give her a number rating. She was sure of it. Trying to calm her hysterical thoughts, she spoke.

"Excuse me, but if you don't mind I need to use the phone. My car has a flat tire."

The housekeeper nodded distractedly. "*Sí, sí*, Mandicita show the *señorita* the phone. *Necessito salir ahora.*"

"I'm sorry. I don't speak Spanish."

Meagan found herself speaking to the air as the housekeeper all but ran outside.

"Hey, wait a minute. I just need to use the phone." Her shouts were futile as the older woman jumped into her car, started it and drove away. Meagan stood on the front porch, staring in shock at the quickly receding white Pinto wagon and the woman who smiled and waved from behind the wheel.

Turning back toward the children, she smiled weakly. "Hi. Would it be all right if I spoke to your parents?"

"Are you our new nanny?" The girl's question caught Meagan by surprise. The new nanny? Meagan felt lightheaded.

"Of course she is, Mandy. Estelle wouldn't have left if she wasn't." The certainty in the boy's voice unloosed Meagan's tongue.

Dreading the answer, Meagan still had to ask. "Are your parents home?"

"No."

Darn it. She knew it. A domestic crisis and she was smack dab in the middle. This was no time to fall apart. She needed to stay calm. Calm. Right.

"Will they be home any time soon?"

"Dad should get here by dinner. That's what Estelle told her daughter when she called." Jason offered the information while looking at Meagan with quizzical blue eyes.

She smiled down at him. It was already late afternoon. The children's father would undoubtedly be home in a couple of hours. Thank goodness. Things were definitely looking up. Moving farther into the hall, Meagan shut the door. There was no sense in standing on the front porch until their father showed up.

"Great. Listen. I'm not your new nanny, but it looks like I'll be sticking around until your dad gets home. Unless there's someone else we could call?"

Jason studied her before answering. Meagan had the distinct impression she was being rated again. "Estelle already tried that when her daughter called. Grandma and Grandpa are out of town and nobody else could watch us."

Why did she get the feeling he wasn't telling her everything? Shaking her head, Meagan tried to ignore the feeling of distrust. Just because her nephew always had something up his sleeve when he used that tone of voice didn't mean this innocent looking little boy did. Then again, her nephew could look pretty angelic, too.

"Okay. Then I guess I'm staying until your dad gets here."

When Jason and Mandy grinned like they'd just won first place in a three-legged race, Meagan figured she was right. The question was: right about what? These two little schemers were up to something, but it was beyond her ability to figure it out. They could not have known that her car would blow a tire in front of their house, so how could she fit in their plans?

ॐ

Adam snapped his briefcase shut and headed toward the faculty parking lot. What a day. These summer classes were a killer. He hated the long sessions crammed into short weeks, with even more grading on the weekends. It was like trying to force-feed his students on an all-math diet. If they remembered half of what they learned he'd be surprised. Still, it was another step toward tenure and security for Jason and Mandy.

"Hey, Adam, hold up."

Impatient to be gone, he turned to acknowledge Eric's call. "What's up?"

Eric jogged up to him wearing his usual shorts and T-shirt, his long hair pulled back in a ponytail. "Just wanted to wish you luck on your interview."

Adam looked around, thankful that no one else was nearby to hear his friend's words. He glared at Eric.

"Hey, don't look so worried. No one heard me. I don't know why you're so uptight about it anyway. It might spark a fire under the board to grant you tenure early."

Or fire him. "An interview isn't going to spark a fire, but a job offer might. So don't say anything."

Eric laughed. "Yeah. You're a savvy guy, Adam."

Savvy? Maybe. He didn't feel savvy, he felt frustrated. He'd taught at the university for five years and still hadn't been offered an endowed chair. That wouldn't be such a big deal except that he knew his classes were some of the first to fill up and often had waiting lists.

He was a good professor and he deserved some security in his job. His children deserved the stability that security would give them. Jason and Mandy were going to have all of the comfort and assurance he had been denied as a child. If it meant being savvy, as Eric put it, then so be it. He'd be savvy.

"Thanks, Eric. I've got to go. The new nanny is supposed to arrive today and Estelle's daughter is due any time."

Eric laughed again, sounding more like an undergrad than an English professor. "You've got a plate full of responsibilities as always. Give me a call when you get back."

Watching his friend walk away, Adam felt a spark of envy at Eric's carefree attitude. Eric didn't have anyone depending on him, no nannies, no housekeepers with pregnant daughters, no one. He could afford to take off for a year at a time and travel, enjoy life.

Enjoy life? Where had that thought come from? Adam enjoyed his life, even if it was full of people who depended on him. Giving himself a mental shake, he headed toward his car. His life was blessed and two of his greatest blessings were waiting for him to come home.

He approached his car and grimaced. With today's temperatures, the Volvo would be like an oven. Unlocking the driver's side door, he stepped back as a blast of hot air hit him. Adam started the car and immediately reached to switch on the air conditioner. This heat wave definitely had its drawbacks.

Smiling, he considered how Jason and Mandy would vehemently debate the issue. They loved to play outside and chase one another around the farm with high-powered squirt guns. The hot summer sun filled them with glee. Adam relaxed as he thought of his son and daughter. Eric might not have anyone relying on him, but then he didn't have two great kids like Jason and Mandy either.

Pulling out of the parking lot, he headed toward Highway 26 hoping that the new nanny had arrived. Estelle was as nervous as one of his students during oral exams waiting for *the call* from her daughter. She acted like her daughter was the first woman to ever face childbirth.

His foot pressed the accelerator as he shot onto the highway. Adam loved driving. He felt so in control, and the power of his car accelerating to freeway speeds was a rush. Caroline would have said it was a man's thing. Caroline. Thankful that thoughts of her no longer caused searing pain, Adam wondered how she would have handled their current domestic difficulties. The knowledge that she wouldn't have taken much interest didn't alleviate his sense of aloneness.

Caroline had been a career army doctor, which required frequent moves for their family. She could never be counted on because if a call came, she was gone. Being a doctor would have been demanding enough, but she had been more than that. She had been a military doctor and her time had not been her own. Their family had never come first.

For Adam it was different.

Jason and Mandy took top priority, before his job, before his friends and sometimes, before his own happiness. It hadn't been that way for Adam's father. He had always put his own concerns above that of their small family. His chief one being where his next bottle of Jim Beam would come from.

Not wanting to dwell on painful memories of the past, Adam reined in his thoughts. The children's nanny, Mrs. Peer, could not have chosen a worse time to decide that she needed to bond with her sister. The woman was in her sixties. He didn't understand why Mrs. Peer had to leave now. Surely another week wouldn't matter. This and other arguments had fallen on deaf ears. Mrs. Peer was not a woman easily moved by the opinion of others. She and her sister were now playing shuttle cock on some cruise liner's deck while he scrambled for someone to care for Jason and Mandy.

His interview for an endowed chair in Illinois had been set up weeks ago. Canceling the trip at the last minute would tarnish his credibility with the university. He would only be gone for a couple of days. When he got home, he would have ample time to deal with his domestic concerns.

The thought held little comfort.

The agency had called and said they were sending someone over, but as of three o'clock this afternoon no one had shown up. Asking Estelle to watch the children was out of the question, considering her daughter's condition. Adam had already promised her time off to be there for the delivery and help out with the baby for a couple of weeks.

Adam gripped the steering wheel in frustration, as everything seemed to press in at once. He would get through this. He would. Just like he had gotten through every other crisis in his life.

Relief surged through him as he neared his home. Jason and Mandy made it all worth it. Their happiness was his reward. As he turned into the driveway, Adam noticed a small red car parked near his mailbox. He'd have to find out who owned it and get it moved. The mail carrier refused to deliver the mail if a vehicle was parked within fifteen feet of the mailbox.

Estelle's car was gone from the driveway. Adam slammed the Volvo to a halt and vaulted from the car. Estelle's daughter must have gone into labor and she'd had to take Jason and Mandy to the hospital with her. He felt terrible. What hospital was it? Surely she would have left a note on the kitchen table. Adam rushed into the house only to come up short at the sound of Mandy's laughter coming from the kitchen.

His children's voices blended with that of an unknown woman. The new nanny must have arrived. Adam's stomach clenched at the husky tones of her voice. Admonishing himself to get a grip, Adam moved to open the kitchen door wider. He wondered what she was like, his new nanny. A mental picture of Mrs. Peer flashed before his eyes. Somehow he couldn't picture the owner of that voice having steel gray curls and a short, squat figure.

Adam pushed the door open and stepped into the kitchen. Neither the woman nor his children immediately noticed him. They were too engrossed in telling silly jokes.

"Why did the elephant cross the road?" asked Jason.

Adam smiled. He'd heard this one more times than he could count. It was one of Jason's favorites.

"I don't know. Why?"

She was young, way too young. Flame-colored curls bounced against her shoulders as she shifted, waiting for his son's response. The Merrick Agency must have been desperate.

They knew his preference for elderly nannies. It made for fewer unforeseen complications.

"Because the chicken had the day off."

The woman burst into a gale of laughter. Small tapered hands came together in applause at his son's wit. Jason puffed out his chest and grinned. Adam smiled in response to Jason's obvious pleasure.

Adam moved further into the kitchen and addressed his son. "I see you've found a new audience for your corny jokes."

"Daddy!" Launching herself from a chair, Mandy flew toward him. Adam opened his arms and embraced his daughter, swinging her in the air and then close to his body for a bear hug. She wrapped her legs around him and he shifted her weight to his hip.

His air left his lungs in a rush as the new nanny stood and turned to greet him. He was barely aware of Mandy sliding from his hold and moving to stand next to the new nanny. She was gorgeous. Emerald green eyes sparkled merrily at him from a perfectly formed face. This was his new nanny? Impossible.

"There must be some mistake." Abashed, he realized he had made the comment out loud when she nodded. Trying to make up for his faux pas, he spoke again. "I mean I usually request a much older nanny. I'm sure the agency had no choice when they sent you."

As soon as the words left his mouth, Adam recognized how terrible they sounded. His nanny's smile didn't falter. In fact, she started to laugh. He felt like a fool.

"Please... I didn't mean that either. I'm just a little surprised. The Merrick Agency has never sent me a cover girl before."

What was the matter with him? Calling his new nanny a cover girl was not the way to set the tone of a professional relationship.

Meagan's smile vanished. Pink crept up her cheeks. "Thank you, I think."

She was embarrassed.

That surprised him. A lovely woman like her should be used to compliments. Maybe the problem was that the compliment came from her employer. She was probably as shocked as he was by what he had said.

"Perhaps we should begin again. My name is Adam McCallister. I'm Jason and Amanda's father."

He offered her his hand. She placed hers in his and Adam felt an inexplicable desire to hold on when they were finished shaking hands.

"It's nice to meet you, Mr. McCallister. My name is Meagan O'Hare and you're right. There has been a mistake."

Chapter Two

Adam stared at Meagan. "A mistake?"

"Apparently your housekeeper mistook me for the new nanny and left before I could explain that I wasn't."

"How could this happen?"

"Well, Dad, you know how Estelle only speaks Spanish when she's upset?"

Adam nodded at his son's words. The entire family knew when Estelle was upset or excited because she walked around the house muttering to herself in Spanish.

"When Meagan got here—"

Adam interrupted his son to correct him. "Miss Meagan."

"Miss Meagan. When she got here, Estelle just left, telling her in Spanish that she was going."

Meagan's smile touched something inside him. "By the time I knew what she intended she was already in her car and halfway down the driveway." Her voice was laced with laughter.

Adam groaned. The sunshine could not dispel his feeling of impending doom. Taking a glass from the cupboard, Adam poured himself some ice tea. He took a sip and then turned back toward Meagan and the children.

"I take it that Estelle's daughter called."

"Yes. Jason said she called long before I arrived and by the time I got here, Estelle was frantic to leave so she could be with her."

Adam couldn't summon up any anger at his housekeeper. He knew she had been emotionally charged over her daughter's impending labor. He should have stayed home until the new nanny arrived. He could have corrected the papers at home and driven them back to his office later. Adam shook off the regret. It was done. The problem now was: if Meagan wasn't the nanny, then where was she? The agency had promised to send someone over today. He was counting on them.

"It looks like I owe you an apology. I'm sure it isn't every day you knock on someone's door and get left in charge of two children you've never met."

Meagan laughed. "You're right about that. It doesn't happen more than once a week, on the outside."

Her teasing humor dispelled some of his gloom. She was taking the situation in stride; maybe he should follow her lead.

"I assume that you came to my door for some reason other than to take charge of my children." Comprehension dawned. Meagan owned the little red car parked too close to his mailbox. "Your car broke down."

She shook her head. "It was a flat actually."

Oh. A flat. "Need help changing it?"

She smiled at his offer and Adam found himself wishing the impossible, that this woman with the beautiful face and infectious laughter was his new nanny.

"No thank you. I've already called some friends. They're on their way over. I would have changed it already, but my tire iron is the wrong size."

"Your tire iron is the wrong size."

Her eyes opened wide at his tone. "Don't blame me. It came with the car."

"Naturally."

She laughed again. "After the day I've had, I guess you could say that. It does seem perfectly natural that my tire iron didn't fit the bolts."

He liked her laugh. It reminded him of a cheerful brook in a quiet dell, bubbly and refreshing. Adam smiled in response. He took a sip of his ice tea.

Mandy scooted her chair closer to Meagan and leaned against her arm. "Miss Meagan is fun. I like her."

Meagan smoothed her hand across Mandy's hair. "I like you too, sweetie."

Something twisted inside of Adam at the exchange. His daughter seemed entranced by Meagan. Had any of Mandy's nannies ever touched her with such tender affection? Meagan O'Hare was a special woman.

"Dad, can we keep Miss Meagan?"

Adam choked on his ice tea. Meagan's eyes twinkled as she handed him a napkin from the basket on the table. Taking it from her grasp, he muttered a quick thank you and wiped at his face. He felt heat in his cheeks. Great. He was blushing. Men did not blush, especially professional men, professors who were used to lecturing in front of large groups. Then again, most men did not have to deal with coming home to find their children in the care of a beautiful stranger and their sons asking to keep her.

"No, Jason, we cannot keep her. Meagan is not a puppy."

"But, Dad, we need a new nanny. The agency one didn't show up. How are you going to go to Illinois if there's no one to watch us?"

Adam sighed. His son was certainly right about one thing: without a new nanny he wasn't going to make his interview.

"I'm sorry about your nanny."

Lured by the sympathy he heard in Meagan's voice, Adam sat across from her at the table. "Thanks. I am, too. I don't know how I'm going to make my plane without someone to watch Jason and Mandy."

She didn't say anything, but gave him a questioning glance, encouraging him to continue. He gave her a brief rundown of the situation, finally starting to relax under her compassionate gaze. It felt good to talk to someone, to vent about his frustration. He rarely allowed himself the privilege.

"That's terrible." She sounded incensed.

Her instantaneous loyalty was balm to his frazzled spirit. "Thanks. I think so, too. What's worse is that the agency that screens my nannies for me was supposed to be sending someone over today."

Meagan's eyes never left his and Adam wondered briefly who this woman really was. Where did she live? Was she married? She wasn't wearing a ring. Unsure why, he was glad.

"Something must have come up." Her voice pulled him from his wandering thoughts.

His hands clenched where they rested on the table. "Unless she's in the hospital, I don't want to hear about it."

His son made a choking noise. Jason's face turned red and ice tea sprayed out of his mouth all over the table. Adam jumped up to pat his son's back. "Jason. Are you okay? What happened?"

Cheeks scarlet, Jason said, "I'm fine. I just swallowed wrong."

Adam rubbed Jason's back. "All right now?"

Jason nodded.

"Good."

Adam sat back down. Catching Meagan's eye, they shared a smile. He could see her thinking, like father, like son. She wiped at the mess with more napkins from the basket.

"What about your housekeeper? Will she be back tonight after the baby is born?"

"That would certainly make things easier, but no. I gave her time off to help her daughter with the baby." Things could not have been more perfectly timed to put him in a quandary.

"What about their mother?"

"She died two years ago."

Meagan's eyes filled with compassion. "I'm sorry." He felt like she had touched his heart with those two simple words. After Caroline's death he had received many platitudes, but few had been as earnestly spoken as her simple declaration.

"Why don't you see if you can get seats for Jason and Mandy? I'm sure that someone at the university could find you competent childcare for the hours of the interview."

Of course. That made perfect sense. "I'll have to call the travel agent right away."

She nodded. "How about if I visit with Jason and Mandy until my friends show up? That way you can make your calls without worrying about them interrupting you."

"That's very kind of you, but I hate to impose."

Her green eyes flashed at him. "It's not an imposition and I wouldn't offer if I didn't want to."

Her quick temper amused him. From the stubborn tilt to her chin, he concluded that she liked to get her way. "Yes ma'am. Thank you." Standing up, he turned to leave the kitchen. "I'll be in my study if you need anything."

"Don't worry about me. Just go take care of your problem."

Right. She made it sound so easy. Maybe it would be. He had the feeling that with this amazing woman, anything was possible. Adam walked down the hall toward his study, vaguely aware that Jason had asked Meagan if he and Mandy could go outside. He didn't hear her answer. His mind was focused on the task at hand: finding two seats on his flight to Chicago.

Adam rapidly punched the buttons to dial the travel agency. *Lord, just two more seats on the plane. That's not a lot to ask is it?*

He waited on hold for a reservation agent. Letting his thoughts slide to his arrival, Adam smiled. Meagan was quite a woman. Cold chills ran up his spine when he thought of what could have happened when Estelle mistook a stranger for the new nanny. God had definitely been watching out for his family.

Meagan had taken the situation in stride. She didn't seem at all upset to have been left in charge of two strange children while his housekeeper tore off to see the birth of her daughter's baby.

Too bad Meagan wasn't a nanny. He could use someone practical like her caring for his children. Oh well, she was too young anyway. Meagan looked in her early twenties, only the laugh lines around her mouth attesting that she was probably near thirty. That wasn't old enough. After one disastrous encounter with a younger nanny, he had learned his lesson: no live-ins under the age of fifty. Not that it had helped with Mrs. Prout. Who would have thought buying light popcorn instead of regular could be construed as a token of his undying affection?

The reservation agent came on the line. Forcing himself to focus on the task at hand, Adam explained his problem. Moments later he was hanging up the phone in disgust. There were no flights available with three seats tonight or tomorrow morning. It looked like he was going to have to postpone the interview. Sitting in his desk chair, Adam closed his eyes and rubbed his hand across his face in frustration.

Out of control. That's how he felt. He didn't like it. He'd worked too hard to order his life. What right did Mrs. Peer have to up and leave him in the lurch? Was there no one he could trust or rely on?

Trust in me.

Lord, it's not that I don't trust you. It's just that right now I need a flesh and blood person to watch my children. Father, show me what to do.

&

"Do you think she's an angel?"

Sheesh, sometimes little sisters could be so dumb. "Of course not. Angels don't wear lime green tennis shoes."

"They could."

"No way. Angels wear white and some of them have wings."

"We prayed for her didn't we? She must be an angel."

Mandy could really be stubborn when she got an idea in her head. "We prayed for a fun nanny, not an angel."

"I guess." His sister didn't look convinced. "She's pretty like an angel though, isn't she?"

Girls noticed the dumbest things. "How should I know? Never seen an angel with red hair, though."

"You've never seen an angel at all and you think you're so smart."

"So. Neither have you."

Mandy didn't argue the point. "Do you really think she's our answer to prayer?"

Jason looked back at Meagan sitting on the porch. She smiled as she watched them.

"Yeah. I told you God would send his own nanny if he got the chance."

"You don't think God'll be mad we didn't tell Daddy about the other nanny's 'pendix?"

"Nah. Dad can be real stubborn sometimes. We needed to do something or we were going to get another nanny just like Mrs. Peer."

Mandy nodded. "I'm glad God sent one that looks like an angel."

&

Meagan stood in the doorway to the study. Patty and Jake had arrived. Jake was already busy changing her tire. Thankfully, he had also brought a full gas can. Her day was finally coming together. By the set of Adam's shoulders she had to assume the same was not true for him. He looked defeated, sitting behind his huge mahogany desk with his head bent as if in prayer.

"Adam."

His head came up, but she couldn't read his expression. The sun's glare coming in through the window behind him cast his face in shadow.

"My friends are here. Any luck finding seats for Jason and Mandy?"

He didn't answer her right away. Shaking his head as if to clear it, he spoke. "What? No. No luck."

"I'm sorry, Adam. I wish there was something I could do."

He stood up and walked around the desk. When she could make out the features of his face, Meagan sucked in her breath. The unhappiness in his expression affected her deeply. His eyes were shuttered as if he didn't want to expose his emotion, but his wrinkled brow and the straight line of his lips told their own story. His hair was disheveled testament to agitated fingers running through it over and over again.

Uncomfortable with the unexpected feeling of empathy that surged through her, Meagan glanced around the study. It was an imposing room, filled with dark wood. Adam went well with his sanctuary. They were both impressive. He had a sense of leashed power about him, like he kept his reactions under tight control. Meagan wondered what it would be like to hear him laugh, really laugh. It wasn't likely to happen right now, not with his interview in jeopardy.

"Adam?"

"I'm sorry. Your friends are here?"

"Yes. I can stay a little longer if you need to make some more calls, though."

"No. Thanks anyway. It looks like the only call I'll be making is to cancel the interview."

The resignation in his tone bothered her. Surely something could be done.

"Isn't there someone else you could call, a friend or someone who could watch the children for you?"

Adam's eyes narrowed. He answered her brusquely. "No one that I would call at this late date."

"But—"

"Look, I appreciate your staying with my children, but I can handle my own problems."

He didn't like asking for help. It should have been obvious. A man who strove to control his emotions like he did would balk at relying on someone else to get him out of a jam.

Tempted to emulate her pubescent niece with a coolly uttered, "Whatever," Meagan bit her tongue to stop the word from coming out. "Fine. Jake should be about done changing my tire. I'll be out of your hair before you know it."

"I'm sorry. I didn't mean to imply that you were in the way. Quite the opposite, in fact. You've gone out of your way for a total stranger and, well, I want to thank you."

Intensity radiated from his gaze. Meagan tried to speak and failed. Clearing her throat, she tried again. "No problem."

Adam followed Meagan into the kitchen where she had left Patty with the children.

"Patty, what are you doing here?"

"Oh, hi, Adam. I'm just here rescuing my friend. All in a day's work you know."

Meagan smiled at Patty's quip. For a confirmed meddler like Patty, it was undoubtedly true. Then the implication of their conversation registered. "You know Adam? Why didn't you say something?"

"Hey, when you called distraught about the car and being left with two unknown short people, you didn't give me any names. It wasn't until we were almost to the farm that I realized you were stranded at Adam's place."

"Oh."

"Patty is my pastor's wife." Adam spoke from behind Meagan.

She jumped. She wasn't aware that Adam had come to stand so close. Moving a step toward Patty she turned to face him.

"Jake and my oldest brother went to seminary together. I've known Patty for years." Was she babbling?

Adam raised his brows in question.

"My brother is twelve years older than me. I was a surprise baby. My parents thought they were long since finished with bottles and diapers." Now she knew she was babbling. She couldn't seem to help herself. Somehow the situation seemed more intimate, and all because Adam knew Patty.

Patty smiled at Meagan in apparent understanding before turning to speak to Adam. "I must say, Adam. If Estelle was going to leave Jason and Amanda with a stranded woman, I couldn't think of a better one than Meagan. She's wonderful with children."

"I noticed. When I got here, Jason was regaling her with silly jokes and she was actually laughing."

Patty beamed at Meagan like a proud mother. This was ridiculous. "Thanks for the vote of confidence, but I'm sure anyone would be charmed by your children."

"Thank you. I agree, but then, I'm their father."

"Well, I'm not related, but I agree too. I've had them both in my Sunday school class and they're terrific." Patty spoke like a woman who knew what she was talking about.

"By the way, where are they?" Adam smiled while speaking. He had a killer smile.

"They went with Jake. Jason wanted to help him change the tire and Mandy was determined to pour the extra gas into the tank."

Adam turned eyes lit with amusement to Meagan. "You ran out of gas too?"

There was nothing funny about it. Couldn't he see that? Evidently not, his eyes were full of unholy glee. "I got lost and by the time I acknowledged that Jake couldn't direct himself out of a paper bag, my low fuel light was blinking."

Meagan got her earlier wish. Adam laughed out loud. His whole body relaxed and his laughter surrounded her like sunshine. "Say no more. Jake has tried to give me directions a time or two."

The warm humor in his gaze mesmerized her.

"And you'd have found the place if you followed them too." Jake's booming voice came from the doorway. "I left Jason and Mandy outside playing. Now those two are smart. They'd have been able to follow my directions."

"Yeah, right. Tell us another story." Adam's easy camaraderie with Jake gave Meagan an idea.

"Patty, I've got a favor to ask you."

"Hey, isn't changing one tire enough for you, woman?" Jake's teasing voice caused Meagan to smile.

"Well, it's not for me really, but for Adam."

"Wait a minute, Meagan. I said I'd take care of my own problems." Adam's glare could melt metal, she was sure of it. Where had that killer smile gone?

Growing up the youngest of five children had taught Meagan a thing or two, and how to ignore glares from irate men was one of them. "I know. I know. You won't ask at this late date, but I will."

"Meagan." The warning tone was there. She smiled. He was an awful lot like her third brother. Aaron always thought he could intimidate her with his voice too.

Patty was watching their by-play with avid interest, if the open-mouthed wonder on her face was any indication. "Adam's nanny agency let him down. Estelle's daughter went into labor, so she's gone too."

Sure that Patty was getting the picture, Meagan smiled reassuringly at Adam. The man needed to learn to ask for help when he needed it, especially when he had friends as loving as Patty and Jake. "Anyway, Adam has to go out of town for a couple of days and he doesn't have anyone to watch the children."

Jake grasped what Meagan was asking immediately. "Sure. Sure. Be glad to help out."

"Now, wait a minute." Ignoring her husband's bewildered stare, Patty went on to explain. "You know we're remodeling right now and I'm not sure our house would be the best place for two active short people."

"Well, yes, but, dear—"

Patty didn't let her husband finish. "Yes. Yes, I know. A friend in need. But there's a much simpler solution than keeping those two active children cooped up at one end of our house."

Adam looked hopeful and Meagan was grateful to Patty for wanting to help. Her gratitude turned to alarm at her friend's next words.

"Meagan why don't *you* stay *here* with the children?"

&

From the look of utter bewilderment on Meagan's face, Adam was sure she hadn't expected her friend to recommend she stay and care for his children. He was tempted to make her pay for her interference by pretending to like the idea. It wouldn't take much pretense either. Having her watch Jason and Mandy would be an answer to prayer.

He couldn't do it though. Meagan looked like she had just swallowed a fish whole. Her mouth opened and closed, but she hadn't said anything.

"I wouldn't dream of imposing on Meagan any more than I already have."

Before Meagan could speak, Patty jumped in. "Oh, I'm sure it wouldn't be an imposition. She wanted to see the sights around here and was planning to stay for a few days anyway. Your house will be a lot more comfortable than mine all filled with saw dust."

"Caring for my children is hardly the same as taking in the sights."

"She loves children, don't you, Meagan?"

Adam was watching Meagan as Patty spoke and he couldn't miss the look of pain that flitted across her features. It was gone as swiftly as it came. "Yes, I do."

He was drawn to the soft vibration in her voice. Meagan hid her emotion well, but he could tell that there was a lot more she would have said if he hadn't been there. The look she gave Patty was ripe with pleading.

Patty ignored the look and swept on. "It was practically her idea anyway. If she'd thought of it, I'm sure she would have offered."

Adam wasn't sure of any such thing and said so.

"Nonsense. Tell him, Meagan."

Meagan stared at him, her mouth parted as if to speak. Adam lost track of the conversation as he stared at Meagan's mouth. Were her lips as soft as they looked? Startled by his wandering thoughts, Adam forced his gaze to her eyes. They had turned dark with emotion. Adam wanted to know what caused this reaction in a woman who had accepted far stranger circumstances with equanimity.

Licking her lips, Meagan spoke. "I don't know. I wouldn't have thought that Adam would want to leave his children with a perfect stranger."

Funny, but her description of herself didn't sit right with him. Adam felt like he'd known Meagan a long time, too long to think of her as a perfect stranger and yet that was an accurate portrayal.

Jake took up his wife's argument. "Nonsense. Adam knows we wouldn't recommend anyone but the best to watch his children. We're a better reference than this agency he uses to find his nannies."

Adam smiled at his friend's words. Jake had let him know in no uncertain terms that he thought Mrs. Peer was a martinet. It was a safe bet that Meagan wasn't anything like her. Adam watched the emotions chase each other across Meagan's face. He found himself hoping that she would agree.

In the corner of his eye, Adam noticed that Jason and Mandy had entered the kitchen. His daughter tugged on his arm to get his attention. "Daddy, is Meagan gonna stay and be our nanny?"

"Just a minute, squirt."

"I want her to stay. She looks like an angel. I've never had an angel for a nanny. It would be almost as good as having a real mommy."

Meagan gasped and Adam's gaze shot back to her face. She looked dumbfounded.

Jason snorted. "I told Mandy, angels don't wear lime green sneakers. She wouldn't listen. I don't care if Meagan's an angel or not. She likes my jokes and I want her to stay."

Adam couldn't stop himself from adding his own plea. "What do you say, Meagan? It would only be for a couple of days."

She fixed her eyes on his and he felt lost in their green depths. He was so preoccupied with the mysteries he saw there that Adam almost missed her answer.

"Yes. I'll do it."

His children whooped in delight. Patty nodded her head like a wise woman endorsing Meagan's decision.

Adam touched her shoulder and felt his fingers heat at the contact. "Thank you, Meagan."

Chapter Three

She was going to drive him crazy. She'd only been there a few hours and Meagan had already upset his neatly ordered life. If he wasn't so grateful to her for watching Jason and Mandy for him, Adam would be tempted to shout. He never shouted.

It had all started innocently enough. Jake and Patty invited everyone out to eat. Jason asked if they could go to McDonald's. He, of course, had said, "No." Meagan had wheedled him into it. There was no other word for it. She wheedled. First, she commented how much she liked their fries. Then she rubbed her stomach saying how she could really go for a Big Mac. Finally, the decision was taken out of his hands when Jake announced they were going to McDonald's. Hungry women had to be fed. The evidence of Meagan's growling stomach could not be denied.

If that wasn't bad enough, here he sat on the couch watching *Chitty, Chitty, Bang, Bang* with Meagan and two children who should have been in bed an hour ago. This time Meagan hadn't wheedled. She'd used logic and guilt.

"You're going to be gone and the children will miss you. Surely they can stay up a little past their bedtime to spend some quality time with you."

Watching an old movie was quality time? Jason and Mandy seemed to think so. They had both nearly gone through the roof when he agreed.

"Dad, this is so cool."

Jason's voice broke through Adam's irritated thoughts. His nine-year-old son snuggled against him eating popcorn. It had been popped on top of the stove. Meagan wouldn't use the microwave popcorn. She said it was unnatural.

It felt good to hug his son.

Mandy yawned and scooted to cuddle against his other side. "Yeah, this is fun."

Adam smiled down at her. His daughter was keeping her eyes open by sheer willpower. Certain she'd lose the battle anytime, he laid his arm around her shoulders to support her head.

Meagan sat on the other side of the white sectional watching the movie. He could have watched her instead of the television screen. Her mobile features displayed every new development in the plot. When the children were tricked into the jailer's wagon, she leaned forward, intent on the screen.

"Don't listen to him. Can't you tell by that nose that he's the bad guy?"

Adam couldn't help it. He laughed. "I thought you said you had seen this before."

Sitting back on the sofa, Meagan pulled a cushion in front of her and held it in her lap. "I have. It's one of my all time favorite movies."

"Then you do know that everything turns out all right?"

She looked at him askance. "Of course I know that, but the children don't."

"Jason and Mandy have seen it before too."

"I didn't mean them."

She meant the children in the movie. "Meagan, they're actors."

"I know that." She sounded offended.

Trying hard not to laugh again, he said, "I'm sorry. I didn't mean to insult you."

Her frown turned to a sheepish grin. "You didn't. At least not much."

He returned her smile.

"I get really caught up in movies."

"I noticed."

She smiled into his eyes and for a moment he was aware of only her. "Mandy looks like she's asleep." Her words brought him back to reality.

He looked down at his daughter. "I think you're right. I guess I should carry her up."

"It won't hurt her to sleep there. She looks comfortable. You don't want to miss the movie. It's almost over."

Agreeing with a nod, he turned his attention back to the TV. When Truly, made up as a life-size doll, started dancing around the castle, Adam thought of Meagan. Stealing another look at her, he smiled at her obvious concentration. He doubted that if he spoke to her right now, she would even hear him.

When the credits rolled he was surprised to see that Meagan was crying. "It had a happy ending."

She looked at him and smiled through her tears. "I know. Isn't it wonderful?"

He was saved from answering that ridiculous statement by Jason. His son shifted next to him and almost tipped over. He was asleep too.

Meagan moved forward. "I'll carry Mandy up, if you can get Jason."

About to tell her that he would make two trips, Adam thought better of it. "Great. Thanks."

Gently lifting Mandy, Meagan just nodded. Adam took Jason up first and laid him on his bed, pulling off his socks and tennis shoes and jeans. Tonight he could sleep in his T-shirt. Tucking the covers around his son, Adam prayed silently before leaving the room.

Meagan waited in the hall. She whispered. "I didn't know which room was hers and I didn't want to go snooping."

Adam nodded and led the way to Mandy's room. He didn't turn on the light, but gave her the same treatment he had Jason in the dark. Meagan had already left.

Meagan was poised to enter her room when he came out of Mandy's. "Good night, Adam."

"Good night, Meagan and thanks...for everything."

ৎ০

Mandy's voice whispering the promised treat of cinnamon rolls for breakfast teased Meagan to wakefulness. Savoring the sweetness of being wakened by the small child, she did not immediately open her eyes. Jason chastised his sister from the doorway for trying to wake her.

"I'm whispering," defended the little girl.

Meagan couldn't hide a smile at this rejoinder.

"I'm awake. Good morning, you two."

"See, I told you she wouldn't mind me whispering."

Meagan laughed aloud.

"Do you like cinnamon rolls?"

When Meagan nodded, Jason smiled his approval.

"Estelle makes the best. But we better hurry or they won't be hot anymore."

"I love cinnamon rolls, but I thought Estelle was with her daughter."

"She is. Daddy pulled some out of the freezer. He said they would be better than cereal for breakfast."

Smart man.

"I agree. So, you two had better scoot. I need to take a quick shower and dress."

Meagan stretched and swung her legs over the side of the bed. Throwing back the patchwork quilt, she put her feet onto the smooth hardwood floor. She had thought the room charming the night before. In the bright light of the sun it was even more so. The old-fashioned furnishings fit the Victorian farmhouse perfectly.

The window was open and cotton curtains fluttered on the breeze. Meagan breathed in the fragrance of lilac and sighed. A rare sense of peace and well-being settled over her. It took her completely by surprise. Perhaps it wouldn't be so bad. God wouldn't give her more than she could handle. She wasn't so sure about Patty.

Moving over to look out the window, the lush green grass and waving corn stalks in the field enchanted her. Brian had often talked of buying a farm, but it had become just another broken dream in their marriage. She could still see Brian's face as the final divorce decree was granted. He had looked both sad and relieved. She had been numb.

Even now, a year later, it was difficult to believe that her husband of eight years had asked her for a divorce. He hadn't had much choice. She would grant him that. Impregnating his legal secretary had forced his hand. After years of infertility tests and painful surgeries Meagan had railed at the injustice of it. She still felt her insides tighten every time she thought of Brian and his new family. Tears pricked her eyes, but she wouldn't let them fall. She had shed all the tears she was going to for her failed marriage and attempt at motherhood.

Without the loving comfort of God and her family, she would have gone crazy. Not that her mother was convinced she hadn't. When she spoke of quitting her job after her sabbatical was over, her family went ballistic. They didn't understand, but she needed change. She needed a new life.

Always having wanted to write, she was determined to give herself the chance. If she couldn't realize her dreams of motherhood, she would pursue another dream, that of becoming an author.

Shaking herself from the reverie, Meagan quickly pulled her things together for the day. A toiletry bag in one hand and her clothes clutched in the other, Meagan made her way to the bathroom. Turning on the shower, Meagan's mind focused on the events of the previous day. Had she really agreed to watch Adam's children while he was out of town? Grimacing, she lathered her washcloth. Patty hadn't given her much choice, that was for sure.

Meagan loved her friend, but couldn't deny that Patty liked to meddle. As the hot water pelted her, Meagan tried to figure out what Patty was up to. Did she think that a few days of watching someone else's children would ease the pain of Meagan's empty arms? It didn't work that way. In fact, spending time with children only seemed to increase the longing in her heart to have her own.

Meagan smelled the cinnamon rolls as soon as she reached the bottom of the stairs. Making her way down the hall she could also discern the pungent aroma of fresh coffee. Sighing with appreciation, she entered the kitchen.

Jason and Mandy sat at the table eating a cinnamon roll and fruit. "Hi, Miss Meagan." Jason greeted her enthusiastically.

"Come sit by me," pleaded Mandy.

"Sure, shortcake, just let me get some coffee."

"I'll get it."

Meagan met Adam's gaze. He was leaning against the counter, his arms crossed. A tan polo and walking shorts set off his dark good looks. What would he look like in a T-shirt and jeans? Probably way too virile.

He thought *she* looked like a cover girl. He must not read many magazines. Anyone could have told him that freckled redheads weren't cover girl material.

"Cream or sugar?"

"What? Oh. Both please. I'm not a coffee purist."

Adam smiled at her quip while stirring cream and sugar into her coffee. Meagan took the proffered cup. "Thanks."

She sipped the coffee. "Perfect."

He smiled and she lost track of her thoughts. "Hey, I can pour coffee and reheat cinnamon rolls with the best of them."

She smiled. "Everyone should be so handy in the kitchen."

Meagan served herself a cinnamon roll. She set it and the coffee on the table next to Mandy. Frosting had made its way to the little girl's cheeks. Meagan picked up a napkin and dabbed at it. "It looks like you've been enjoying your pastry."

Mandy gave Meagan an adoring smile. It reminded her of Mandy's words the day before. *Having a nanny who looked like*

39

an angel would be almost as good as having a real mommy. Meagan's heart had responded to the longing she heard in Mandy's voice. It was so close to her own yearning. How could she have refused to watch the children after that?

Meagan finished wiping Mandy's cheek and tapped her on the nose. "Done."

"Thank you, Miss Meagan."

Meagan smiled before closing her eyes briefly to thank God for her food. Remembering the peace she had felt upon waking, she thanked Him for that too. When she opened her eyes, she found Adam looking intently at her.

"You really are good with children."

"Thanks. That's what the pastor says back home. It's his excuse for asking me to spend every spare moment involved in Children's Ministry."

Adam laughed and Meagan's heart did a somersault at the sound. This was one man she had to watch out for. He was too appealing for her peace of mind. She wasn't in the market for a man. Brian's betrayal had left her gun-shy and she wasn't up to target practice to overcome her fear.

When Jason and Mandy finished their breakfast, Adam sent them upstairs to brush their teeth. He poured himself a cup of coffee and joined Meagan at the table. He had a sheaf of papers in his hand.

"I have to leave for the airport in about an hour, so we'd better go over this now. I want to make sure we have time for me to answer any questions before I go."

Meagan eyed the papers in his hand. "You're only going to be gone two days, right?"

"Yes. We discussed this yesterday."

She nodded.

"Fine, then." He pulled out a list, studied it for a moment and then began going over the other papers in his hand. "I put the emergency numbers, my cell-phone number and the hotel where I'll be staying on this sheet." Adam placed the page from a yellow legal tablet in front of Meagan. The information was neatly listed with the hotel's name and address at the bottom. Adam waited for Meagan to say something. He was more organized than the admin in her department at Design Tech.

"Um, this is very clear. Thank you."

Apparently satisfied, Adam nodded and checked off the first item on the first paper he had pulled out. "This is my itinerary, including my flight number and time."

Meagan looked down at the white papers emblazoned with a travel agency's logo. She quickly scanned the pages, feeling like Adam expected her to do so.

After checking off the second item on his master list, he laid another set of papers in front of her. "This is Jason and Mandy's schedule."

The computer-generated daily agenda looked a lot like Meagan's time management table from Design Tech. He had specified the times the children got up, when Meagan should get up, what time to eat and their bed time. It included a separate schedule for each day, indicating the children's television programs and what hours they were on, quiet time for reading before bed and recommendations for activities.

"You'll notice that I left most of the daylight hours blank. You can fill them in later when you've decided what excursions you are going to go on."

Looking up, Meagan caught Adam's expectant gaze. He thought she was going to schedule each day down to the minute? "Uh, Adam, I don't always know what I want to do until I decide to do it. If you're concerned about me taking Jason and

Mandy somewhere you don't want them to go, I can go over the suggestions Jake and Patty have given me with you."

"That won't be necessary. Jake and Patty wouldn't send you anywhere you couldn't take Jason and Mandy."

"Great."

He checked off the next item on his original list. "This is a summary of the children's medical records. It includes any allergies they have."

Meagan's head was starting to spin. "I'll make sure I read it."

"Good. Now, one last thing."

There was more?

"I've written down Jake and Patty's address and phone number along with those for the church. You probably already have them, but then again..." Adam let his voice trail off.

Meagan felt herself blushing. "I got lost because of Jake's lousy directions, not because I didn't have their address."

"Of course." His expression was bland. "Can you think of anything else you need?"

How about a way out of spending three days in the bittersweet company of his two adorable children? "Not a thing, thanks."

"Okay. Then here's some money to cover incidentals and eating out."

Meagan looked at the wad of bills in Adam's hand. "Why don't we just settle up when you get back?"

"Nonsense. I really appreciate you watching Jason and Mandy for me. I don't want you spending your money taking them around the sights."

"But Adam, that's more money than I'll need to take them to a few tourist attractions with me."

"I expect to pay your way too, Meagan. It's the least I can do."

The implacable line of Adam's mouth made her realize any more argument was futile. "That's not necessary, but I can see that you're convinced it is." Meagan took the money from Adam's hand. "Do you want me to keep a record of the money spent and receipts?"

Adam looked shocked. "Of course not."

"I just thought that since you like to keep such good records..." Meagan trailed off, waving at the stack of papers on the table in front of her.

"One has nothing to do with the other. How you spend this money is your concern. I'm trusting you with Mandy and Jason. I'll certainly trust you with my money."

℘

Exhausted from spending the day sightseeing with two active children and Patty, the overzealous tour guide, Meagan relaxed on the porch swing. Tucking her legs under her, she sipped on a glass of fresh lemonade. The tangy flavor revived her drooping eyelids. Frothy pulp clung to the glass and her lips.

"You make a mean lemonade, Patty."

"So, I've been told." Patty grinned. "Will you look at them?"

Meagan obeyed her friend and looked out across the yard at Jake and the children chasing one another with squirt guns. "It's hard to believe they have the energy. I'm pooped."

Patty gave Meagan a mocking smile. "Yeah, I can tell. We practically had to drag you back to the car after the zoo."

"What do you expect? We walked more today than I usually do in a week. When I asked you to show me the sights, I didn't mean all in one day."

Patty laughed. "Poor Meagan, you need to get more exercise."

"Hey, I exercise. But I'm not a triathlete. I'm a design engineer."

"I thought you were a writer."

Meagan sighed. "Yeah, well being a writer isn't going to pay the bills. The editor I met with at the conference told me they aren't publishing fantasy children's books right now. I'll probably have to go back to Design Tech when my sabbatical is over."

"I thought you said you wanted to make a clean break with your old life."

Trust Patty to cut right to the heart of the matter. She did want a clean break from her life that had been filled with stress for so long, she could barely remember what peace was like. "I do, but it isn't easy. I need to eat, you know."

"You can't pursue your writing when you're putting in sixty-hour workweeks at Design Tech."

"I know that, but what choice do I have?"

"Why don't you move up here?"

"You think the computer companies around here are any less demanding than Design Tech?"

"No, but being Jason and Amanda's nanny would be."

Meagan stared at Patty. Could she have heard her right? "You think I should stay as the permanent nanny?"

"Yes. It's the ideal position for you."

"You've got to be kidding."

"No, I'm not. Now listen to me, Meagan. You need a change of scenery. I'm worried about you. Your brother tells us that all you do is eat, sleep and work."

"Not anymore. Since I went on sabbatical, I haven't worked at all."

"You're always busy on the computer when I call. Don't tell me you're not working."

Meagan didn't reply immediately. What could she say? It was true. Some days, she wrote for twelve hours straight. The next day, she would end up throwing out half of what she had typed, but it didn't matter. She needed something to fill her mind and her days.

Patty moved over to sit next to Meagan on the swing. She put her hand over Meagan's. Her voice was gentle when she spoke. "Honey, your divorce was final a year ago. It's time to move on with your life."

The words stung. "I have moved on."

"No, you've gone into hiding. You fill your days with work so you don't have to think."

"What makes you such an expert?"

"Believe it or not, you aren't the first divorced woman I've counseled. It kind of goes with the territory."

Meagan sighed heavily. If it were only the divorce, maybe she'd be over it by now. Her failed marriage didn't haunt her dreams at night, her desperate desire to be a mother did.

"Patty, I know you mean well, but being a nanny is the last thing I want right now."

Patty didn't speak for several moments. She just sat there, patting Meagan's hand and rocking the swing. "Being a nanny may not be what you want, but it might be just what you need."

Meagan just shook her head.

Patting her hand one last time, her friend stood up. "You want to write?" The words were brisk.

"Yes."

"Then you need a job that gives you time to write. I know that not only did Mrs. Peer have weekends off, but she was only responsible for the children for part of the day."

The schedule did sound good, but it wouldn't compensate for the emotional turmoil she would be in watching someone else's children. "I don't want to be a nanny."

"Nonsense. You've never been one. Besides, caring for two charmers like Jason and Mandy will be a breeze."

"Yeah. Right. Those two have unplumbed depths, I just know it."

"That will make the job all the more interesting. You don't want to get bored, do you?"

"What I don't want is to be a nanny."

"You keep saying that."

"Because it's true."

"Why don't you want to be our nanny, Miss Meagan?" Mandy stood looking at her with soulful eyes after asking her question.

She hadn't meant to hurt the little girl's feelings. "It's not that I don't want to be your nanny, it's just that I don't want to be anybody's nanny."

"It's the same thing." Jason's voice was laced with accusation.

Meagan turned toward the little boy. His stance was defiant and his eyes were fierce. "We prayed for you and now you don't want to stay. What did we do wrong?"

The words echoed Meagan's cry to God when she discovered her infertility. It felt like a knife twisted in her heart.

46

She couldn't allow Jason to feel that it was his fault. He and Mandy had told her that they considered her their answer to prayer.

"You didn't do anything wrong. It's just that I'm a design engineer, not a nanny."

"But you could be a nanny." Mandy moved forward and climbed into Meagan's lap. Meagan's arms automatically went around the little girl to give comfort. "You would be a really good nanny. I know it."

Meagan couldn't speak around the obstruction in her throat.

"If you leave, Dad will hire someone just like Mrs. Peer and she won't help me build Legos and she'll make Mandy give away Caroline." Mandy was very attached to a rag doll named after her mother. Meagan wished she could say a few choice words to Mrs. Peer on the subject after learning that the other woman had threatened to throw away "that dirty bundle of rags".

Meagan could feel Mandy stiffen at her brother's words. "I don't want to give away Caroline."

Hugging the little girl tighter, Meagan said, "No one is going to make you give up Caroline."

"Please, Miss Meagan. Please stay and be our nanny." Jason's defiant face crumbled to reveal the vulnerability of the little boy's heart.

"Jason, I can't promise that I'll stay."

"Will you think about it?"

Unable to deny the pleading in his voice and Mandy's tense expectancy, she nodded. "Yes. I'll think about it."

Letting out a war whoop, Jason jumped off the porch. "Cool."

Mandy snuggled closer to Meagan. "Thank you, Miss Meagan. I knew you couldn't leave, not when God sent you."

Looking over Mandy's head, Meagan didn't miss the look of complacency on her friend's face. She gave Patty a glare, which the other woman blithely ignored.

That night as Meagan prepared for bed, she considered taking the position of nanny for Adam's children. Patty made the logistics sound too good to be true. Meagan had to admit that right now, pay wasn't as important as having a comfortable place to live and time to write. Could the benefits make up for the way her heart constricted with longing when she saw Adam hug his children and knew she wouldn't have any of her own?

On the other hand, maybe being a nanny was as close to motherhood as she was going to get. Would it be enough? Jason and Mandy needed her. They believed God had sent her in answer to their prayer. Maybe he had.

Getting up to pace the room, she considered the alternatives. She could go back to Arizona, her sixty-hour workweek, and her lonely apartment. Or, she could move out here and take the job as Adam's nanny. Living in a house with other people again was tempting. Meagan was a social person. She didn't mind being alone occasionally, but she didn't like living that way. Undoubtedly the result of growing up in a house full of siblings.

Could it be God's will for her to care for Adam's children? Was she worthy? He had not allowed her to get pregnant. Maybe there was a reason.

Whenever God closes a door, He opens a window. Meagan could hear her mother's words as if she were standing there next to her. Was God opening this window? If he was, did she want to crawl through?

Chapter Four

Adam sat on the bed in his hotel room and dialed the number again for the farm. He'd tried several times already and had only gotten the answering machine. He had even called Jake at the church office. Jake informed him that Patty and Meagan had taken the children sightseeing. Patty wasn't home yet either. Leaving another message, he hung up the phone in frustration.

He wanted to talk to Jason and Mandy. He missed them. He wouldn't mind talking to Meagan, either. Funny how her succinct questions helped him keep things in perspective. After a telephone conversation they had the night before he felt more clear-headed about this job opportunity than he had since the call had come requesting he fly out for an interview.

It didn't make any sense. The better he got to know the woman watching his children, the more he realized how differently she handled life. She was one of those free-spirited, unscheduled people. Adam shuddered at the thought. Still, there was something about her that drew him.

Hungry, he picked up the phone and dialed room service. He wasn't about to leave and miss Meagan's call. As he took a bite of his steak, the phone rang. Trying to chew quickly, he picked up the receiver. "Hello."

"Adam, is that you?"

He swallowed. "Yes. It's me. I was eating."

"Do you want me to call back later?"

"No!"

"Are you sure? It wouldn't be any problem."

He didn't want to wait to talk to her and the children. "No. Really. I can wait to eat. I'd rather talk to the children now."

"Okay. I'll put Jason on the line. He's right here."

He'd wait to talk to Meagan until after he'd spoken to the children. "Fine."

"Hi, Dad."

"Hi. What did you guys do today? I tried to call before and you were gone."

"I know. You left six messages."

Adam groaned. Six? He didn't realize he'd called that many times. "So what did you do today?"

"Um, we went to OMSI. The new exhibits are really cool. But before that, Meagan took us to the mall. I didn't know malls were tourist attractions, but she says she never goes to a new place without visiting their mall."

Malls were tourist attractions? "She must really like the Portland area. There are plenty of malls."

"Yeah. She and Patty took a long time deciding which one we were going to go to."

Sounded like a waste of time to him. "Did you have fun?"

He was surprised when his son answered in the affirmative. "Yes. Meagan let us go to all the toy stores. Then we got to watch her and Patty get makeovers. It was kind of cool, like somebody painting on their faces. Meagan looked really different though. They put some goop on her that covered her freckles."

Amused at his son's description of make-up, Adam chuckled. "I miss you, buddy."

"I miss you too, Dad. I can't wait to see you tomorrow night."

"You won't see me tomorrow night, Jason. I'll be getting home way past your bed time."

"That's okay. Meagan said we could camp out in the living room and wait up for you watching movies."

"She did, did she?"

"Yeah. I love you, Dad. Mandy wants to talk to you."

"Okay. I love you too, Jason."

Seconds later his daughter's voice came over the line. "Hi, Daddy. Is it hot there? Meagan said it's really hot in Illinois and humid. What's humid?"

Adam laughed. "It's when there's a lot of water in the air."

"I thought that was rain."

"Humidity is different from rain. It's like the steam from a shower, but you can't see it." How was Meagan handling Mandy's inquisitive nature?

"We're going to have a campout in the living room tomorrow night."

"I know. Jason told me."

"Meagan said we could make beds on the floor. She called them pallets. She answers questions as good as you do, Daddy."

"I'm glad to hear that, squirt. Do you think I could talk to her now?"

"Yes. I'll get her. She went to make dinner."

"Thank you, honey. I love you."

"I love you too. Lots."

He smiled at his daughter's sweet declaration. It was worth whatever it took to give her and Jason a protected childhood. They would never be exposed to the ugly side of life as he had been. Jason would never have to listen to a drunkard's ramblings. Mandy would be spared seeing a woman trodden down by life to the point where her eyes rarely focused on the world around her, including her young son.

"Hello?"

"Hello, Meagan. I just wanted to touch base with you and make sure everything was going well."

"We're having a marvelous time. Jason and Mandy are incredible. You know, at the science museum *they* explained the exhibits to *me*. It was great."

Adam smiled at Meagan's enthusiasm, but the smile left his face when he remembered her plans for them tomorrow night. "Have you found the schedule helpful in determining your plans each day?"

His question was met with silence.

"Meagan?"

"Um, Adam, I think there's something I should tell you."

"What?"

"I'm not big on schedules."

No kidding. "Really?"

"Yeah. I, um, I haven't really looked at the schedule much."

"I wondered. Perhaps that's why you planned a campout in the living room with Jason and Mandy to wait for my arrival. I won't be getting home until three hours after their bedtime."

"Jason and Mandy know what time they go to bed, Adam. I didn't have to look on the schedule to figure that out."

She sounded offended. "I see." But he didn't. Then why was she planning to let them stay up so late when he could just as easily see them in the morning?

"We're having the campout because your children miss you. Mandy even said she'd rather have you here than her Caroline doll." Meagan spoke in measured tones, like she was lecturing a student who wasn't very bright.

He felt terrible. Of course they missed him. He missed them too. "I guess it would be all right. I'm not sure I understand why they're sleeping in the living room, though. Why don't you just watch movies?"

"Because there's more adventure in a campout of course."

Of course. Why hadn't he thought of that? Then again, why would he? He did not spend his time trying to fill his life with adventure. In fact, the opposite was true. He liked his neat and ordered existence. No surprises meant no heartache and disappointment.

∞

Meagan couldn't concentrate on the movie. Adam was due any minute. All she could think about was the reluctant promise she had given Patty and the children to discuss the nanny position with Adam. She clung to the fact that Adam probably wouldn't hire her. He was so ordered that he would undoubtedly be more comfortable with someone else.

Twisting a strand of hair around her finger, Meagan recalled his chagrin when she informed him that she hadn't referred to his schedule since he left. She popped a kernel of buttery popcorn in her mouth and felt it dissolve on her tongue. No, Adam definitely did not like her unscheduled approach to life.

He didn't understand the need for variation in the routine of life. Jason and Mandy did. They told her often how much more fun she was than Mrs. Peer. The feeling was mutual. Her growing affection for them was the main instigator for her rash promise to apply for the position of nanny.

The fact that Adam's voice over the phone turned her insides to jelly played a part in both her reluctance and her desire to stay. How could she be so affected by a stodgy professor? Adam was everything she wasn't, but that didn't stop her heart from beating a quick tattoo when she played his messages on the answering machine. Even when she played them the second time...to make sure she hadn't missed anything.

Meagan was barely aware of the sound of tires crunching gravel when Jason and Mandy sped by her to the front door. "Daddy's home!"

Meagan sprang off the couch and followed the children. She stood behind Mandy as Jason threw open the front door. Adam had just stopped his Volvo. The driver's door swung open and he stepped out. He stretched. The floodlight illuminated taut muscles as Adam reached above his head.

Jason and Mandy sprinted off the front porch and across the small patch of lawn to Adam's side. "Hi, guys." He swept them both into a bear hug. "Boy, I missed you."

Crickets sang in the stillness as Adam embraced his children, the look of rapture on his face testimony to how deeply he had missed them. Familiar feelings of longing curled through Meagan. In a flash of insight, Meagan realized that she didn't just want her own children. Right now, she wanted to be part of the scene before her. She wanted to be held tightly to Adam's chest and have Mandy clinging to her legs.

Her mind was going. She barely knew Adam and his children. The desire to become a mother was so strong that she was projecting her feelings onto Adam's family. Unable to deal with her irrational emotions, Meagan turned around and made her way back into the living room.

She moved around the room, straightening the soft blankets, picking up stray kernels of popcorn and tidying the pile of stuffed animals Mandy had wanted to bring to her campout. What was the matter with her? If she was going to stay on as Adam's nanny, she would have to get control of her hormones.

A sexy voice was one thing. Being tempted to throw herself at a near stranger and share in a joyous family reunion was something else entirely.

She could hear Adam and the children calling her. Taking a deep breath and expelling it, Meagan prepared to greet Adam.

"There you are." Adam looked rumpled from his travel, but no less appealing. If anything, his tousled hair and wrinkled trousers made him more approachable.

Stop it, Meagan mentally chided herself.

"Where did you go, Miss Meagan? You were right behind us." Jason spoke from next to her.

"I thought I'd pick up a little bit." She ruffled his hair. "I didn't want your dad to think we'd torn apart the living room for our campout."

"Daddy wouldn't care. He's nice, Miss Meagan. He never yells at our nannies."

Meagan smiled at Mandy's pronouncement. She was fairly certain that their previous nannies would not have dreamed of turning the sofa into a makeshift tent either.

"Mandy's right. I wouldn't mind. I don't mind. I'm just glad to be home."

Meagan's gaze met Adam's. His happiness was palpable. She felt a smile spread across her face. "I can tell."

He returned her smile and Meagan's breath caught in the back of her throat.

"This is our campout," Jason announced. Adam seemed to take in the white sectional draped with bedding, the popcorn bowl that was nearly empty and the water bottles full of ice water with one sweeping glance.

"Looks like fun. What movies did you watch?"

Meagan listened with half an ear while Jason and Mandy chattered excitedly with their father. How was she supposed to bring up the issue of her staying? She'd never applied for a domestic position before. Was there a different type of application process? After her reaction to the scene between Adam and the children, maybe she should forget about it. Still, a promise was a promise. Her mind was in too much of a muddle to deal with it right now. She'd wait until tomorrow.

Suddenly aware of the silence around her, Meagan looked up to find three sets of eyes focused on her face. Jason and Mandy looked expectant and Adam looked like someone had just punched him in the stomach.

"What? Why are you all looking at me?"

Adam cleared his throat. "Mandy just said... I mean Jason thinks..."

He was speechless. What had she missed?

"We just told Dad that you're going to stay and be our real nanny."

Meagan stared at Jason. "You said what?"

"Miss Meagan, you promised."

Mandy sounded near tears. Shoot. If she didn't get things under control soon, she was going to ruin Adam's homecoming.

"I promised to talk to your dad about it and I will."

Mandy's smile returned. Jason nodded with approval, but Adam still looked like he'd been blind-sided. She smiled at him apologetically. "I couldn't help it. Patty and the children can be very persuasive."

He blinked. "Patty?"

"Yes. She seems to think that it's the ideal solution for both of us."

"She does?" The puzzled look on Adam's face was almost comical. Meagan wanted to reassure him that she wouldn't insist on staying, but she couldn't say much more in front of the children.

She just nodded and then turned to speak to Mandy and Jason. "Okay, troops, the agreement was you'd greet your dad, hug him silly and then go to bed. How are you two at keeping your promises?"

Jason and Mandy immediately threw themselves at Adam and gave him more enthusiastic hugs. He scooted them upstairs to brush their teeth before escorting them back to their "camp". Meagan listened to Adam praying with his children from the doorway of the living room.

He kissed them and tucked their blankets around them before turning off all but one small light.

"Night guys."

"Good night, Daddy. I'm glad you're home."

Adam brushed his fingers against Mandy's forehead. "Me too, squirt."

Mandy smiled and snuggled deeper into her blankets. He walked by Meagan and she followed him to the kitchen.

"Want anything?" he asked as he got himself a glass of water.

She shook her head. "No thanks."

He sat down at the table and she joined him, sliding onto the cold wooden seat. "I'm sorry you got put on the spot like that. I guess I should have realized they wouldn't leave it to me to tell you."

Adam played with his water glass, turning it in his hands. "To say that I'm surprised would be to put it mildly. I was under the impression that you were here on a mini-vacation, not looking for a job."

"I was. Like I said, Patty can be pretty persuasive, not to mention Jason and Mandy."

"I still don't understand this thing with Patty. She's never made a recommendation before about my nannies."

He obviously didn't know Patty as well as she did. "You may as well get used to it. Patty likes to meddle."

"You'll have to forgive me. I'm having a hard time taking this in."

Meagan felt bad. "I can imagine. We don't have to discuss this tonight. As a matter of fact, I would rather wait until tomorrow."

Adam's shoulders relaxed. "That would be great."

Meagan stood up. "I'll go to bed then."

As she went to open the kitchen door, Adam's voice stopped her. "Meagan."

She turned her head. "Yes?"

"You've told me that Patty wants you to stay and I can see that Jason and Mandy want you as their nanny, but I'm not sure what you want. Do you want to stay?"

Meeting Adam's eyes, Meagan saw the question there. She needed to make a decision. Suddenly, it all seemed very clear. Life was full of risk, but it seemed to her that the greatest risk of all was to miss out on living it.

"Yes, Adam. I do."

Chapter Five

She wanted to stay. Adam shook his head, trying to clear it. Meagan O'Hare, cover girl turned temporary babysitter, wanted to be his children's nanny. That thought had played havoc with his sleep the night before. He swung his desk chair around and looked out the window of his study. Acres of cornstalks waving peacefully in the summer breeze against a backdrop of vivid blue sky did nothing to settle his agitated spirit. What was he supposed to do?

Turning back toward the desk, Adam lifted a pen and began to write. Making a list of pros and cons would allow him to make the decision based on logical alternatives. He started with the cons. The biggest one was his undeniable attraction to her. She wasn't a professional nanny. She didn't like schedules. She was too young, although to be fair this could be included with his first point.

Shifting his pen to the other side of the paper, he concentrated on the benefits of hiring Meagan. Under the pro header he wrote that Meagan was good with children and active in children's ministry, so she must have some experience. He made a note to ask her whether or not she taught Sunday school or had any other experience teaching. Jason and Mandy wanted her to stay. So did Patty.

The scratching of his pen ceased abruptly. Why did Patty want her to stay? He picked up the phone and dialed Patty's number. She answered on the third ring.

"Hello?"

"Adam McCallister here. I'm sorry to call so early, but I have a question for you."

"No problem. Shoot."

"What's going on?"

"I beg your pardon?"

Adam grimaced. He hadn't meant to be so blunt. Strangling the pen he held, he spoke again. "Meagan wants to stay on as my nanny. She said that you and the children talked her into it."

"It's marvelous the way she's bonded with them so quickly. Don't you agree?"

"I'm not sure."

"Come, Adam, what could you possibly have against Meagan?"

"I don't know that I have anything against her. I just don't know anything about her."

"Have you asked?"

"Not yet." Meagan had agreed to meet him in his study when she was finished with breakfast and her quiet time.

"I'm sure she'll answer any questions that you have. She is a very forthright person."

"Meagan can't tell me why you've decided that she's the answer to my dilemma."

"You've had a hard time keeping a nanny. Jason and Mandy need more security than a new nanny every few months."

True enough. He'd had six different nannies since Caroline died. He didn't understand it. Hiring elderly women through a professional agency should have guaranteed some measure of stability, but it hadn't. "Are you trying to tell me that Meagan will be more long term than my other nannies?"

Patty made a strange sound at the other end of the line, but when she spoke her voice was even. "Yes. That is exactly what I'm trying to say."

"Why?"

"Because, well, because Meagan is a dedicated person."

A dedicated person. "Is that all?"

"No. Listen, Adam, I know you like to make your decisions based on a list of alternatives, having weighed every option, but sometimes you've just got to do what feels right."

Adam looked down at the paper before him. Patty knew him well.

"When I realized that Meagan had gotten stranded at your farm, it was obvious that God had intervened. Meagan is wonderful with children and would be very good for Jason and Mandy. They'll be good for her too. It's the perfect situation all the way around."

Something like certainty settled in his heart at Patty's words but he fought against it. Impossible. "Thanks, Patty. I'll let you know what I decide."

"Just don't make your decision without praying. Okay?"

"You have my word."

Adam hung up the phone and stared sightlessly at the bookcase on the wall opposite his desk. The smell of lemon furniture polish attested to Estelle's cleaning frenzy while waiting for her daughter to go into labor. He straightened the notepad in front of him, aligning it symmetrically with the edge of the desk.

God had intervened.

Was it possible? She had made a "camp" out of his living room. If he hired Meagan, his life would be filled with chaos. She was unscheduled, free-spirited and everything he avoided in a nanny.

She was also kind and generous, smart and totally delectable. Adam groaned. How could he hire a woman who reminded him that he was more than just a father, but that he was also a man?

Adam bowed his head in a prayer laced with desperation. *Are you sure, Father? Are you absolutely sure?*

൭

Mandy watched Meagan finish cleaning up the breakfast dishes. Daddy had told her not to worry about it, but she washed them anyway. She was an angel. Maybe not an angel from heaven, Jason could be right. She was still an angel. She cuddled when she read stories. Meagan gave kisses when she tucked Mandy in. Daddy had to hire her. Meagan was perfect.

"I'm going to go upstairs for some quiet time. I'll see you two later." Even her voice was perfect. It was soft just like it was supposed to be, just like a mom's voice would be.

"Okay, Miss Meagan. When are you going to talk to Dad?"

Mandy waited anxiously for Meagan to answer her brother's question. "Right after I'm done praying." Meagan's smile made Mandy happy. It was a special smile, just for them.

Meagan left the kitchen and Mandy turned to her brother. "Let's go on the back porch."

He would probably argue. Jason always argued with her.

"Okay."

Whew. That was easy. Mandy sat on the porch swing, liking the feel of the cool slats against her legs. She loved summer when the air was warm and she could smell the flowers and fresh cut grass. Setting the swing in motion, she turned her head to gaze intently at her brother.

"Do you think Daddy will hire her?"

"He better. God sent her and if he doesn't hire her, I bet God will be mad."

Mandy didn't like the idea of God being mad at Daddy. "Do you think God would be really mad?"

"Yeah. Dad's smart though. He'll figure it out."

"Are you sure that Meagan's the answer to our prayer?"

Jason stared at her like she was dumb. She hated it when he did that. Mandy glared at him. This was important, but Jason didn't know how important. He thought they had just prayed for a nanny. Mandy didn't want a part-time nanny anymore. She wanted a full-time mom. So she prayed in her heart that God would send someone who could be both.

"Of course she's the answer to our prayer. What else would she be? Even Mrs. Patty said God intervened."

"What does intervene mean?"

"I don't know for sure, but I think it means that God did it."

"Oh. Good."

"Yeah." Jason jumped up. "Race you to the barn!"

ဆ

Adam shifted his gaze from his desk to the door when Meagan entered. Moving restlessly around the room, she looked at his books, the pictures on his desk, at everything but him. She wore a tie-dye T-shirt tucked into white denim shorts, appearing more like one of his students than a professional nanny.

"Perhaps you would like to sit down." His voice sounded more forceful than he intended.

Her head jerked up, but she didn't sit down. She held up a picture of Caroline. "Is this your wife?"

"Yes, that was taken the year before she died." The ache he usually felt when discussing his dead wife was missing. Maybe the wound had finally closed.

"You must miss her." Her voice was husky with sincerity.

"Not as much as I used to. Time really does dull the pain."

"Yes, I know."

He waited for her to explain and when she didn't he expected her to ask how Caroline had died. He found that most people were interested in the details when they learned he was a widower. When she merely sat down and shifted her gaze to the paper in front of him, he realized she wasn't going to ask. He wanted to tell her.

"My wife was in an automobile accident. Caroline was in a coma when she arrived at the hospital and she never woke up." The words were stark, but they symbolized months of heartache and dwindling hope.

Meagan's eyes misted. "Oh, how awful."

Her immediate empathy washed over him, strangely comforting. Offering her a tissue, he watched in surprised wonder as she sniffed a couple of times and blinked her tears back. Meagan was crying for him. She barely knew him and yet she was moved to tears by his two-year-old tragedy. He wanted to comfort her, let her know that it didn't hurt anymore.

"It's been two years."

"Is that long enough?"

Adam surprised himself when he answered. "Yes. At least for me." It was true. It had been long enough. He had come to terms with Caroline's loss. The thought was sweet. His pain had disintegrated into the memories.

"I wonder if it will be for me." She whispered the words absently, her eyes focused on her lap. He doubted she even realized she had spoken them aloud. Had she suffered death as well? Was her empathy born of her own pain? Not comfortable prying, Adam changed the subject.

"I called Patty this morning."

Meagan's head snapped up. "What did she have to say?"

"That she thinks I should hire you. That God intervened."

Meagan stared at him. She squirmed in her chair and the fragrance of vanilla assaulted his senses. It was so different from the cloying scents that some women wore, or even the antiseptic hospital smell he always associated with Caroline, that he was momentarily startled. Her voice jarred him back to reality. "God intervened?"

"Uh, yes. Patty is convinced that your arriving on my doorstep was divine intervention."

Infectious laughter took him by surprise. "That sounds like Patty."

Adam felt his lips curve into a smile. "Yes."

"I imagine you would like a little more information to go on for your decision."

Grateful that she understood his need to interview her, Adam looked down at his list before speaking. "Why don't you start by telling me something about yourself? I know your name, that you're good with children, and little else."

Meagan was silent for a long moment as if she was carefully formulating her response. "I'm twenty-seven. I am currently on sabbatical from Design Tech. I'm a design engineer and hopeful author. I write children's fiction. As a matter of fact, I was returning from a writer's conference in Seattle when I got stranded in front of your farm. I'm divorced. I don't smoke and I don't drink. I have several nieces and nephews, whom I watch frequently. I believe I have also mentioned that I am involved in many areas of children's ministry at my church in Scottsdale."

She was divorced. "Do you mind telling me what happened with your marriage?" Adam could hear the hesitancy in his own voice. He hated asking such a personal question, but the answer was important.

Her eyes met his and held. "My husband's secretary came up pregnant. Not a tragedy in itself, but evidently Brian was the father. This complicated things. Naturally, she wanted to be married to the father of her child. The fact that he was already married to me posed a minor inconvenience easily handled by a couple of attorneys and a judge." Meagan's light tone belied the pain behind her words and the devastation she must have experienced.

They said that every divorce had two sides. He couldn't fathom Brian's. The man was a loser. Feeling an irrational desire to defend and protect Meagan, Adam's body grew rigid with anger. "Your ex-husband needs a psychiatrist if he preferred another woman to you."

Her eyes widened and color stole into her cheeks. "Thank you. That's pretty much what my family thinks too."

"So, do you mind if I ask why an engineer slash hopeful author wants the position of nanny to my children?"

"Patty told me I was hiding in my work. I decided that she was right. I often put in sixty or more hours per week at Design Tech. It's time for a change. I want to pursue my writing and Patty is convinced that working for you would give me the time to do so."

Adam inclined his head without saying anything.

"She told me that you only require part-time care for Jason and Mandy?" Meagan turned the statement into a question.

"Yes. When Estelle is here, I require care for Jason and Mandy from eight o'clock in the morning until two in the afternoon. If I'm not home from my classes by then, Estelle takes responsibility for them."

"That sounds great."

"Yes, well, there is one other requirement."

Questioning him with a raised brow, Meagan encouraged him to go on.

"The nanny homeschools the children."

"Homeschool? You mean teach?" Meagan's voice sounded faint.

Adam smiled at her response. "Yes. Don't be too concerned though. I plan to put them in private school in the fall."

"So, I won't have to teach them?"

"Actually, yes. We school through the summer."

"Why?"

"I want my children to have stability and order in their lives. Changing the routine in summer would disrupt that."

Meagan stared at him like he had just announced that he expected Jason and Mandy to work for their room and board. "You're kidding."

Irritation filled him. "No. I'm not."

"But Adam, that's ridiculous. It's summer. Most school children take a summer break, even those in year-round school."

"I'm not concerned with most children. We are discussing *my* children."

Meagan's eyes narrowed and she fixed him with a stinging glare. Words tumbled out of her mouth in an accusing rush. "No wonder *your* children have been so thrilled the past few days. They actually got a break in their *routine*."

"Don't glare at me like I'm abusing them. I explained why we maintain our schedule in the summer."

"You think that order and stability can make up for joy and spontaneity?"

Why was she so adamant about this? "School is over by lunchtime, there is still plenty of time in their day for fun."

"I've seen their schedule."

Adam was stung. He replied with sarcasm. "I'm surprised you looked at it."

"How could I help it? You went over it and every other one of your multiple lists before you left for Illinois."

Adam felt the lash of her words. She made him sound like a man obsessed rather than the organized person that he knew himself to be. "I merely tried to address all contingencies."

Meagan sighed. Her anger was gone as quickly as it had come. "I could tell."

A reluctant smile tugged at the corners of his mouth. "Yes, well maybe I did go a little overboard."

Meagan returned his smile and Adam felt the tension drain from him. "When you pulled out the daily schedule with blank spots for me to fill in with my excursions, I thought I was going to die."

"It might surprise you to know that my previous nannies appreciated my attempts at helping them to remain organized."

Meagan's eyes glittered with amusement. "I can imagine."

"Meaning?"

"Jason and Mandy told me about Mrs. Peer. She sounds like the kind of person who would thrive on an hourly schedule."

Adam nodded. Yes, Mrs. Peer had been very structured, never surprising him in word or deed. That is until she left to bond with her aging sister. "Mrs. Peer fulfilled all of my requirements for the caregiver of my children."

Meagan's smile vanished. "I think you should know something. Your children have some of their own requirements for a nanny."

This wasn't exactly a bolt from the blue, but it hurt to know that they had told Meagan rather than him. "Such as?"

"Both Mandy and Jason have expressed concern to me over having another nanny like Mrs. Peer."

"I'm not surprised." It made sense. They had never bonded with Mrs. Peer. He couldn't really imagine anyone bonding with the woman. A part of him believed that her leaving was a blessing. "They obviously want you and you're nothing like her."

"Thank you. I will take that as a compliment."

Adam chuckled. Meagan was a unique equation, one he was not sure he could solve with all of his deductive abilities.

"About the homeschool. Is that going to pose a problem for you?"

"I've taught Kid's Church for the last eight years. I guess I can handle it."

He smiled wryly. "Your enthusiasm is overwhelming."

Meagan's pert nose scrunched like she'd just bit into a sour apple, but she had agreed. From what he could tell, when Meagan agreed to do something, she did it, and did it well. Jason and Mandy's glowing reports of their three days with her attested to that.

"I suppose you'll want to talk salary and days off."

"You mean you're going to hire me?"

"That is what you wanted?"

"Yes, but I'm nothing like Mrs. Peer. I probably don't fit your requirements for a nanny at all. I can't believe you're offering me the job."

Adam shrugged his shoulders. "Who am I to argue with divine intervention? But I do want to be clear on one point. You will be giving up your job at Design Tech, correct?"

"Yes."

"Good."

ᏸ

And that was that. Adam hadn't had any more questions for her, though he had been full of advice. The man really needed to loosen up a little.

Meagan contacted Design Tech's personnel department and informed them that she would not be returning. Most of her things had been in storage since the divorce and she decided to leave them there for the time being.

It was one thing to take a risk and another to throw caution completely out the door.

⁊

Meagan found the schoolroom easily. It was downstairs, just down the hall from the kitchen. It looked like a mini classroom with a teacher's desk and two student desks. The walls were covered with educational posters and corkboard. Meagan smiled at the efforts of the children. Pulling the teacher's manuals from a drawer, she sat down to study them.

Two hours later, she was impressed and only slightly terrified. Sunday school was one thing, teaching a full curriculum was something else entirely. She was still reeling from the fact that Adam had agreed to hire her.

Lord, you really do have a sense of humor, don't you?

It was downright hilarious when she thought about it. Adam, the order guru had hired her, the queen of spontaneity to be his nanny. Even funnier, she had accepted the position, summer school and all. Meagan scanned the notes she had taken and felt the stirrings of excitement. The curriculum *was* really good. She would make school fun for her charges.

Meagan got up and went outside. The perfectly manicured lawn stretched out invitingly. Slipping off her sandals, Meagan rubbed her toes into the lush green grass. Where were Jason and Mandy? Had Adam told them she was staying? She searched the yard, looking for them. Maybe they were playing with their water blasters in the front yard. Jason said there were better trees to hide behind in the front. Smiling to herself, Meagan wandered around the house. She didn't see them, but the barkdust-covered flowerbeds caught her attention.

Something was missing.

Flowers.

There were no flowers in the beds.

Perfect.

Meagan went in search of Adam. She tracked him and the children down in the barn. He was busy talking to the farm manager and Jason and Mandy were busy talking to the cow. Meagan laughed.

Adam stiffened and whipped his head around. Catching his eye, she motioned that she'd like to talk to him. He nodded and turned back to the farm manager. After another brief spate of conversation, Adam dismissed the other man. Jason and Mandy abandoned the cow.

"Miss Meagan, Daddy said you're staying!" Mandy hugged her fiercely.

Hugging her back, Meagan agreed. "Yep. I'm staying. I'm going to teach you and take care of you and maybe even squeeze a little fun in there somewhere."

Adam raised his brows. "Are you sure there will be time for fun with my exacting schedule?"

"I'm creative. I'll manage." She winked at him. Her heart constricted when he winked back. She almost forgot what she wanted.

"I looked over the curriculum and I'll need some things for class tomorrow."

"Sure. Whatever you need."

"Great. Where's the closest nursery?"

Adam's eyes widened. "What exactly is it that you need?"

She shifted her glance to Jason. He was petting the cow. "Oh, just a few seedlings. They're for science."

"I'll take you. I have to drop the children off for a birthday party and then we can go."

"Why don't you just give me directions? I don't want to impose on your time." And she wasn't sure she wanted Adam along to question her purchases either.

"It wouldn't be an imposition at all. Besides, I don't want to risk you getting lost and ending up as someone else's nanny."

Meagan felt her face heating. "I'm sure I can find my way, provided you give better directions than Jake."

"I can't guarantee it, so I'll just have to take you. Can you be ready in fifteen minutes?"

Defeated, Meagan nodded.

The nursery exceeded Meagan's expectations. Grower's tables full of seedlings stretched at least fifty feet to the back wall. Above them hung baskets of blooming fuchsias in purple, white and magenta. One entire wall was covered with rose bushes in two-gallon buckets. Meagan was drawn to their heady fragrance. Putting her hand out, she caressed one velvet crimson petal.

"They're beautiful."

"Yes. They are." Adam's voice was so close to her ear, he startled her. She looked up and was arrested by the way he intently gazed at the roses. "I wanted to plant roses along the front of the house. They were my mother's favorite flower."

"Why don't you?"

Adam cleared his throat and said something she couldn't quite hear.

"What did you say?"

"I said, I don't know how."

"But, Adam, you're a farmer. It shouldn't be that much of a stretch to grow roses."

"I'm not a farmer. I'm a math professor."

"The semantics are not important. You live on a working farm, you're a farmer."

"I don't know anything about farming. That's why I hired Eduardo."

"I don't understand. Why did you buy a farm when you know nothing about farming?"

"For Mandy and Jason." He turned away, but not before she saw the look of pain in his eyes. "I wanted them to have an environment they could explore and experience while growing up. They need room to run and play without their next door neighbor hearing every time they flush the toilet."

Adam's voice had take on a bitter edge.

"Did you grow up in an apartment?"

He grimaced. "You could say that."

She remained silent, waiting for him to go on.

"I grew up in a series of dingy, run-down buildings. Half the time our hot water didn't work, or the heat, you get my drift."

Meagan ached for the child Adam had been. "It must have been tough, but you've given Jason and Mandy a wonderful environment to grow up in."

"Yes."

"There's no reason you can't have the roses now. I'll teach you all you need to know. I'll even help you plant them."

"You don't have to do that, Meagan. Gardening is not in your job description."

"I'll consider it one of my perks."

Adam turned his intense gaze to her. "It's my turn to ask a question."

"Ask away."

"How did you take care of your garden working sixty hours a week?"

Meagan turned back to the roses, bending down to sniff a large yellow blossom. "The garden went with the house and the house went to Brian."

"You can't be serious. What judge in his right mind would award Brian the house when he was caught in adultery?" Adam's voice was harsh with anger.

"The judge didn't award him the house. I gave it to him. He needed the room for his new family." Would Adam understand, or would he question her sanity like her family had?

Meagan felt the gentle pressure of Adam's hand on her shoulder, pulling her back around to face him. He placed his finger under her chin and lifted until her eyes met his. Their warm brown depths were void of condemnation and filled with sympathy.

"You did it for the child, didn't you?"

"Yes."

He let her go. "You have a very tender heart." Adam didn't say it like her family did, like it was a weakness. Adam made her tender heart sound like a strength. Meagan smiled.

"Okay, about those rose bushes."

They finally agreed on ten plants after a vigorous argument. Adam wanted them all to be the same color for uniformity. Meagan thought a rainbow of colors would look prettier. They compromised by choosing three of the crimson roses, three Queen Elizabeths which were a lovely soft shade of pink and four plants with white blooms. Adam wasn't thrilled, but he had agreed after Meagan reminded him that she was the expert on roses.

Adam didn't exactly stomp off to arrange delivery of the new bushes, but he came close. She wanted to laugh. She headed toward a grower's table heavy with petunia seedlings in every imaginable shade. They would be perfect for the science class she planned tomorrow. Carefully examining each plant, Meagan had selected twenty by the time Adam returned.

"What are all of these for?"

Adam wasn't done being angry that she'd dared to disagree with him over the rose bushes. "Our science class tomorrow. We're doing a lesson on plants."

"You may not have noticed, but you only have two students."

Adam's sarcastic tone grated on Meagan's nerves. "Of course I noticed, but I want to do things right."

"I see." His tone of voice said that he clearly didn't. "Wouldn't vegetables have more long-term teaching potential?"

"Not necessarily. Besides, if we need to study the growth habits of vegetables, we have acres of corn."

"Yes. Right. It looks like I'll have to get something to put these in."

Meagan wanted to laugh. He was definitely used to getting his own way. It was time he learned more about variety and compromise. Adam had the look of a man whose carefully laid plans were crumbling around his feet.

He hadn't seen anything yet.

Chapter Six

"If you two are done munching, it's time to start school," Meagan said when she was finished with her breakfast.

Adam paused on his way out the door, to smile approvingly.

"Do we have to? Can't we take a vacation?"

And get her fired? Besides she had promised Adam. "I should say not. Aren't you two just dying to find out what your ears and the ocean have in common?"

"What do you mean? My ears are small and the ocean is big," said Mandy, pulling on the lobe of her right ear. Meagan found it hard not to laugh.

"Come to school and I'll explain."

"You two be good students for Miss Meagan. Got it?"

"Yes, Daddy, I've got it." Mandy didn't sound thrilled at the prospect.

Adam turned to leave. Meagan called after him, "Should we expect you back about two, then?"

"Yes."

Terrific. Today would be the perfect opportunity to teach Jason and Mandy that school could be fun. It could even be spontaneous.

∞

"Hi, guys."

Meagan jumped as if shot. What was he doing home? It was barely eleven o'clock. She knew her face registered dismay. Meagan had wanted to have her outdoor science class a fait accompli when Adam returned that afternoon.

Summoning a smile, she returned his greeting. "Hi, Adam. You're home early."

"Yes. I had a feeling I should check on school, it being your first day and all. So, this is your science lesson?"

Meagan flinched at the censure in his voice. What was he thinking? He knew she intended to plant flowers for class today. He had bought them.

"Yeah, Dad, isn't it great?"

"What are you learning?"

"Meagan's teaching us botany," replied Jason, putting emphasis on his new word.

"Yeah, and Daddy, did you know that school can be outside sometimes? Especially in the summer. Meagan said so." Mandy was oblivious to the look of disapproval on her father's face.

"Can it now? Well, that's good to know. *Especially in summer.* I'm sure my students would be thrilled by this particular piece of information. Have you spent your entire school day planting flowers outside?"

The muscles in Meagan's neck tightened painfully and she gripped her small spade with rigid fingers. "Of course not. We had our Language Arts, History, Geography and Math in the schoolroom. We moved outside for our science lesson."

Adam didn't say anything.

"I thought that since the sun is so scarce up here, the children should enjoy it while they can." She swiped her hands on her shorts and got angrier when she saw the streaks of dirt she had left on the denim.

"I think that is an excellent idea."

"I'm so glad you approve."

"I'm sorry I came on so strong when I first got here. I mistook the situation."

That was obvious. "Yes, you did."

"I apologized, Meagan. I don't know what else to say."

"You didn't trust me."

"I barely know you."

"You know me well enough to leave your children in my care."

He paused for a moment, obviously letting the words sink in. "Good point. I'll try not to jump to conclusions again."

Meagan felt her anger melting. That was the thing with her temper. It flashed and then it fled. Adam really did look penitent. "Okay."

"Did you think the children's feet needed more exposure to the sun, too?"

His question caught her off-guard. So did the way he eyed her bare feet. It made her toes tingle. "I like to go barefoot and the children wanted to try it, so I let them."

"Ah."

"I suppose that's not something you do."

"No, but it does look like fun." Then he shocked her by removing his own socks and shoes. He *could* be spontaneous.

"Cool, Daddy's goin' barefoot too," exclaimed Mandy.

"Doesn't it feel neat?" asked Jason.

"Yes, it does. If I go change in to shorts, do you think I could join your class on botany?" he asked, turning to Meagan.

Meagan didn't respond immediately. Her toes were still tingling, among other things.

"It's fine if you don't want me to. I have plenty of work to keep me busy." He lifted his briefcase as proof of his statement.

Meagan found her voice. "We'd love to have you join our class. Wouldn't we?"

"Yeah, and then you can answer some questions too. Meagan sure asks a lot," said Mandy.

"Great, I'll be back in just a few minutes. Don't ask anything really interesting until I am."

When Adam returned a few minutes later, she had Jason and Mandy digging holes for seedlings.

"Okay, I'm ready for class."

Most teachers would love to have such an attractive student. In his white polo and khaki walking shorts, he looked like a model for GQ. Meagan was mesmerized by the muscles on his legs. He hadn't gotten those teaching math.

"Do I pass inspection?" he asked in a lazy drawl.

Meagan could feel herself blushing when he caught her staring. She didn't answer, but tried to divert his attention with the lesson. "We're learning about the parts of a plant. Jason, why don't you explain to your father the purpose of the root structure."

"Um, the roots go into the soil and then take the nutrients from the soil to help the plant live and grow."

"Very good, Jason. Now Mandy, would you like to explain to your father why we plant the seedlings with lots of water?"

"It helps the plants grow. And, um, all plants need water. Baby plants need lots of it because they are babies and need extra water to grow larger."

"Good, now perhaps Mr. McCallister, you would like to explain why we are planting these petunias on the south side of the house."

Her question appeared to have caught him off-guard. His head snapped up and he turned startled eyes to her. Finally, he answered, sounding unsure. "Petunias must like a lot of sun?"

"Yes, they do." She smiled, wanting to put him at his ease. She felt bad tormenting him after he had already admitted to her that he knew next to nothing about gardening, but the temptation had been more than she could resist. Particularly after his less-than-enthusiastic view of her science class. "Now, would you like to help us plant some?"

"Sure." He knelt down by the flowerbed and took one of the seedlings. Meagan watched as he looked to see what his children were doing, and then he tried to emulate them.

Jason and Mandy were gently breaking open the root ball and placing the seedlings in the holes, patting a special mixture of soil and fertilizer around them.

He tried to open his root ball, but small sections of the delicate roots fell to the ground. His seedling looked like a plant with a strange tail hanging from it.

"Here, give that to me. I can't stand to see you mangling it," said Meagan, laughing.

Adam laughed with her. Her fingers brushed his as she took the seedling from him. An urge to prolong the contact surprised her. He watched her plant it and his intense scrutiny unnerved her.

"You really are an expert."

"Thanks."

He turned his head toward where Jason and Mandy were planting more seedlings. They were both so intent on what they were doing that they were lost to their surroundings.

"You certainly know how to make the classroom a fun place to be."

"That was the idea."

Mandy finished planting her last seedling. "I can't wait to see them. What color do you think these are?"

"I don't know. That's half the fun of buying mixed colors, you don't know until they bloom. It adds the spice of mystery to gardening."

"Well, it's all a mystery to me," Adam admitted.

"Daddy, you are so silly."

"Dad, I bet Miss Meagan will teach you. She knows everything about plants," chimed in Jason, having finished with his last seedling.

"Not everything, Jason," Meagan corrected.

"As a matter of fact, Miss Meagan has already promised to teach me about rose bushes."

"I'm always willing to take on a new student, but all of my students have to learn their lessons in order. Are you ready for lesson number one?"

Adam smiled at her. "What's that?"

She lifted the garden hose and sent an icy spray dead center in his chest. "The first lesson for any of my students is how to cool off."

He sprang forward and caught her hands around the garden hose. Grinning at her, he forced the spray backwards and soon Meagan felt like she'd been caught in a rain shower.

Her hair hung down limp and her clothes were wet, sticking to her skin.

"Get her, Dad," yelled Jason, just as she managed to wrest the hose and her hands from his grip.

With a quick turn, Meagan doused Jason. Mandy screamed with laughter until Meagan got her too. She ran squealing across the yard for the safety of the house. Suddenly Jason came out from the barn, where he had run to escape the hose, carrying a huge water blaster.

He pumped it and then aimed for Meagan. His aim was good and he got her smack in the face. Sputtering and laughing, she lost her grip on the hose. Adam immediately grabbed it and doused Mandy again before she got inside. She turned, and laughing, launched herself at his knees. He went down.

"Hold him while I spray him," yelled Meagan.

"I'm trying, hurry," Mandy yelled back.

Like a flash, Meagan had the hose again and was alternating its spray between Adam and Jason. Adam finally got smart and turned off the water to the hose.

Meagan cried foul before dropping the limp hose onto the grass. "Everybody cooled off?"

Jason and Mandy agreed immediately, but Adam just stood staring at Meagan. Meagan looked down at her clothes, which seemed to cling to every feminine curve. She groaned. At least she wasn't wearing white. Impulsiveness had its drawbacks.

"I wouldn't use cool, cold or even mild to describe it." Adam spoke in a husky drawl that sent shivers down Meagan's spine.

Looking to escape his heated gaze, she turned away. "All right children, time to clean up. March, one, two, three, four." Meagan, head high, led Mandy and Jason into the house.

Adam's laughter followed her.

ℝ

Meagan concentrated on cutting the small shapes out of the brightly colored construction paper. She felt cold air blow across her ankles as Patty's central air conditioning kicked on. "I still can't believe you installed central A/C when you remodeled. You live in Oregon for goodness sake."

"It feels nice today though, doesn't it?"

Meagan had to agree. Adam didn't have air conditioning at the farm and the house, especially upstairs where they slept, was stifling. It got better when she turned on the fan Adam had placed by her window, but she still had trouble falling asleep at night. They were having another heat wave. She had to admit that the heat wasn't the only thing keeping her awake at night. Images of a tall, dark professor flitted across her brain, making her toss and turn in the darkness.

"You know, I really appreciate your help with Vacation Bible School, Meagan. There never seems to be enough volunteers and I end up cutting out craft projects until three in the morning."

"No problem, Patty. I'm doing a lot less than I was back in Scottsdale."

"You couldn't tell that by me. In the month since you started coming to church with Adam, you've taught Sunday school twice, filled in for the children's choir director and agreed to chaperone the Friendship Club's visit to the homeless shelter, not to mention all you're doing for Vacation Bible School."

"Stop it. You're making it sound like I'm doing too much. I might have to back out of VBS."

Patty shuddered. "Don't even think it."

Meagan laughed. Patty knew she wasn't serious. "Speaking of the homeless shelter. How many children are planning to go?"

Patty tied off a string of multicolored beads before speaking. "About ten or twelve, including Jason and Amanda. Jake wants to go too, so there will be three adults. Have you asked Adam if he wants to come along?"

"No. I haven't had the chance."

Meagan didn't want to admit that she'd been avoiding Adam. When he got home she high-tailed it for her room, using her writing as an excuse. The man was just too attractive and too irritating. When they were together, they argued. It was always the same. Adam wanted everything structured and Meagan chafed against the bounds imposed on her by his schedules.

"You'd better ask him soon, if for nothing else than to make sure he doesn't mind Jason and Amanda going."

"That won't be a problem. Adam told me before he even hired me that he trusted your and Jake's opinion for excursions. The only issue might be that it's during their school hours, but I think that I'll just call it a field trip."

The phone rang before Patty could remark on Meagan's statement.

Patty came back to the table. "That was Jake, he's going to be late. Again. It's probably for the best. Dinner's going to be late anyway."

Looking at the large pile of craft cut-outs that were still undone, Meagan had to agree with her friend. "I'd better call the farm and let them know I won't be home in time for dinner."

"Don't worry about it. I told Adam you were eating with us."

"Thanks." They worked in companionable silence for several minutes.

"So, are you glad you decided to stay?"

"Yes, I'm glad I stayed. I'm getting a lot of polishing done on my manuscripts."

"What about Adam?"

Meagan didn't look up from her cutting. "What about him?"

"Are you two getting along?"

"We get along great." She paused. "When we're not fighting."

Patty laughed. "Admit it. You like the man."

Meagan put down her scissors and paper. She looked at Patty. "Yes. I like him, maybe too much. It's just that he's so honest and caring. And he's such a good father."

"You won't get any arguments here. What are you going to do about it?"

"Nothing. I'm sure he doesn't feel the same way and besides, the worst thing I could do is get involved my employer. If it didn't work out, I wouldn't just lose Adam. I would lose Jason and Mandy too."

ՏՌ

Adam leaned back in his chair and stretched. It had been a long morning at the university. He would have liked nothing more than to come home and just relax, but finals for his summer classes were coming soon and he hadn't written one of them. Hearing a light tap on his study door, he looked up to find Meagan framed in the doorway.

In the few weeks since she'd been there, Meagan had added a new dimension to their lives. Jason and Mandy loved school and he found himself looking forward to meal times when she would share her wit and sometimes outlandish views on life with him. Unfortunately, she kept busy with her writing the other hours he was home. She rarely sought him out, so he was momentarily surprised by her presence. "Hi, Meagan. Can I do something for you?"

"I just wanted to talk to you about an excursion Patty has planned for the Friendship Club. I agreed to chaperone, but it's during school hours."

He smiled. This should be easy and they wouldn't end up in one of their frequent "discussions" about the children. "Will you be taking Mandy and Jason?"

She nodded. "I planned on it. I thought it could be a field trip."

He stood up. "That sounds fine. Anything else?"

"No. That's all." She turned around to leave.

He moved around his desk to follow her. "Do you know where Jason and Mandy are? I need to talk to them."

She looked back over her shoulder before going out of the room. "They were in the kitchen helping Estelle can spicy pickles the last I checked."

"Great. I made an appointment to meet with their teachers and tour their new school. I wanted to tell them about it."

She spun back around and he almost collided with her as she stepped back into the room. "Are you sure that's what you want to do?"

Okay, keep it cool. There is no reason to believe that just because she has that martial light in her eye that there is going to be another argument. Be diplomatic. His little silent lecture did nothing to ease the tension building in his shoulders. "It's time they had the stability of a regular school routine in their lives."

She crossed her arms over her chest. "They already have a routine."

Rubbing the back of his neck, he gave in to the inevitable. "I know that, but they need the additional security of the normalcy that comes from attending school."

She plopped down in a chair. "Why?"

Sighing, he stepped around her to lean against the desk. "I'm not going to argue with you again, Meagan. It seems like lately that's all we've been doing and I don't understand it. We both love my children and want what's best for them."

"Maybe we just have different views on what's best."

Adam rubbed his temples. As one of his students would have said, that was a no-brainer. The problem was Meagan thought that he should change his views too often for comfort. Didn't she realize that *he* was the parent? "Yes, and for some reason you keep forgetting that I'm their father and you're their nanny."

She tipped back her head so that she could look him in the eye. The fire shooting from her eyes told him that whatever she was about to say was going to singe him. "If you want my opinion, they have too much schedule and not enough time to just be children."

He sighed with exasperation. "They have all afternoon to play. It's hardly a sacrifice for them to spend their morning schooling."

"You've said that before."

"Yes, I have. So, why are we having this discussion?"

"Because I don't agree with you. I know their schedule, Adam. I take care of them. And yes, I think that having one that strict year round is too much of a sacrifice. Where is the space for adventure and the opportunity to be lazy once in a while? They don't even sleep in on Saturday because you always have something scheduled for their morning. This isn't boot camp; it's their childhood."

Her words hit him like a sledge hammer. He pushed away from the desk and walked around it to stare out the window. Was he pushing Jason and Mandy too hard? In his quest to give them security, was he robbing them of their childhood? "I didn't think I ran a boot camp. I thought I was giving them a stable home, unlike what I had growing up."

Her hand on his arm startled him. She had moved to stand next to him and he could feel the remorse flowing off of her. "I'm sorry, Adam. I know that you want the best for Jason and Mandy. Maybe if you explained just what it was about your childhood you're afraid of repeating with them, I'll understand better."

"I'm not afraid of repeating anything. I'm nothing like my father." He didn't mean to sound so defensive. It was simply that of all the mistakes he might make with his children, the one he wasn't guilty of was being like his father.

"Adam, I did not accuse you of being like your father. Please, just for once, listen to me." Her voice was edged with exasperation and she shook his arm for emphasis.

"I do listen to you."

"No, you don't. You have your mind all made up and I talk until I'm blue in the face, but you don't hear anything I say. It's driving me crazy."

It sounded so much like something his wife used to tell him that he blurted out, "Caroline used to say the same thing."

She dropped her hand from his arm and took a step back. "It's a common complaint among wives."

"I guess maybe it is, but not nannies. None of my other nannies told me I drove them crazy."

"Don't feel too bad. Just about everyone thinks I'm crazy." She smiled at him, clearly trying to lighten the mood. That was one of the things about Meagan that took some getting used to. One minute her temper flared and the next she was teasing him out of his bad humor.

"My family thought I was nuts to quit my job as a computer engineer to start writing. I won't even tell you what they said about my moving up here to become your nanny. If you weren't a friend of Jake and Patty's I'm sure my mom would have been up here on the next flight available."

He could imagine. If Meagan had been his daughter, he would have questioned her sudden move to Oregon too. Still, she had shown a lot of grit to move away from everything familiar. "It took courage to pursue your dream."

"Thanks, but you should have seen the look on the car salesman's face when I traded my Mercedes in for an Escort."

He could indeed picture it and the thought made him smile. "I wish I had been there." She had done it again, teased him out of his anger. "I really do want what is best for the children."

"I know you do."

If she hadn't sounded so sincere, he might not have explained. He stood up and walked over to the bookcase. He trailed his hand along the spine of the books, pulling one out to look at briefly and then putting it back, trying to think of the words to begin. "My dad was an alcoholic. Alcoholism is just a

91

word until you have to live with it. It carries a heavy price tag. He couldn't hold down a job and we spent our life going from one broken down place to another. We had no stability until he died of liver disease. We never moved again."

She made a sympathetic noise and reached out to squeeze his hand.

"We stayed in the same derelict apartment until I graduated from high school. I worked hard in school and got scholarships to attend university. My mom remarried another alcoholic. They died in a car accident. He was driving. His blood alcohol level was so high, it was a miracle he wasn't already in a coma. I was twenty-one and almost ready to graduate from college. I kept right on working and never looked back."

"Adam, I'm so sorry." She sounded like she was going to cry. He hoped not. Something about the idea of Meagan crying twisted his gut.

"It's okay. It was a long time ago. So, now you understand why I want stability in Jason and Mandy's life."

She looked at him for a long time before speaking. "Adam, I think every parent wants stability for their children, even ones who had an easier childhood than yours. Don't you think though, that you could take a little break from the routine once in a while? When was the last time you took a vacation? You need to have some fun in your life."

"I know how to have fun."

"Whatever you say."

He glared at her. "How did we end up with you lecturing me again?"

She shrugged. "I don't know. You're just lucky, I guess."

"You know, Meagan, you would have made a great mother." She had the lecturing part down and the tenacity of any mother intent on getting her point across.

"Thanks."

He was curious. "Do you mind my asking why you and Brian never had children?"

"I'm infertile."

Chapter Seven

Adam felt like Meagan had just sucker punched him. He sat at his desk, replaying the stark statement in his mind. *She was infertile.* She would be an incredible mother. How could this be true?

Meagan picked up the picture of Caroline with Jason and Mandy taken right after his daughter's birth. She studied it for a long time without speaking.

"How can I envy a dead woman?" The torment he heard in her voice hurt. "I wanted to be a mother. We tried so hard. Can you imagine how I felt when I found out that Brian had gotten another woman pregnant?" Meagan's eyes glistened with tears, but she blinked them back.

He knew the anguished thoughts that would have gone through his mind. "You felt betrayed by both Brian and God."

Meagan's eyes widened. "Yes. Exactly. I went through so much pain trying to get pregnant, and then this woman who committed adultery with my husband conceived. I couldn't believe that God would let that happen."

"You stayed committed to Christ, even in your pain." Adam wanted to reach out and comfort her, but didn't know if he would stop at comfort. His relationship with her was already dangerously close to going over the line between an employer and his nanny. "How do you feel now?"

"I don't know. I try to trust God and believe that there's a divine purpose in my infertility. It's just so hard and my heart won't give up hoping."

Adam didn't say anything. There was nothing to say. Meagan had lost out on the dream of her life and she still smiled, still laughed and still argued with him over his schedules. "You're an incredible woman."

Meagan pulled a lock of her hair forward and twisted it around her finger, like Mandy when she was contemplating a new idea. "Thanks, but I think you're overstating the case. Sometimes I don't feel like much of a woman at all. There's something about not being able to bear children that makes you feel that way."

Adam couldn't believe what he was hearing. "That's ridiculous. Not being able to have children doesn't make you any less of a woman."

"I know that here." Meagan pointed to her head. "But I have a hard time believing it here." She pointed to her heart.

80

"Miss Meagan! Miss Meagan! Miss Meagan! You'll never guess!"

Meagan slid the cereal box back onto the shelf and turned to face her excited charge. She looked beyond Mandy, jumping up and down in front of her, to Jason's grinning face.

"What's going on?"

"Daddy's taking us on a 'scursion."

"We're leaving right after breakfast." Jason's voice was at least two decibels higher than normal.

"Where are you going?"

"We're going to Salem. All of us, that is, if you're game." Adam spoke from behind her. "You did say the children needed a vacation."

His body was much too close to her for comfort. Her heart started to pound. "What about the university?" She tried to edge away from him.

"I don't have any classes, so I took the day off. Estelle packed us a picnic lunch. I thought we could go to a park or something. Will you come?"

He was doing the unthinkable. He was being spontaneous. How could she refuse? "Yes, that would be wonderful."

She felt his gaze take in her tank top and shorts, straying to her legs and Meagan felt heat travel up her skin. "Bring a sweater, in case it gets chilly."

Meagan nodded. She made another effort to move back, desperate in her need to distance herself from this man who inspired her body to react so strongly. The counter's hard surface pressed against her backside. "Adam?"

He smiled at her and then moved back a step, leaving barely enough room to squeeze by him. The intensity in his gaze was doing strange things to her breathing pattern. Scooting around him, she took her cereal to the table. Would he have kissed her if Jason and Mandy weren't in the room?

Did she want him to? This kind of thinking was only going to lead to trouble. Sitting at the breakfast table, she tried to concentrate on her cereal. It didn't work. Her eyes were drawn to him like a thirsting man to an oasis in the desert.

"Daddy, why is Miss Meagan staring at you? Do you have something on your chin?"

Meagan wanted to sink under the table. Adam smiled and gave her the sexiest wink she had ever seen.

"I don't know, why don't you ask her?"

She shot him a look of irritation. It was his fault. He could at least have the decency to look scruffy in the morning, instead of so dang gorgeous.

"I'll get my things." She leapt out of her chair and escaped upstairs. She heard his rich chuckle follow her down the hall. She quickened her pace. How was she going to handle the long drive to Salem? She thought about feigning sleep. She didn't want to be caught staring again. Think scenery, she told herself.

She needn't have worried about fighting her urge to ogle Adam in the car. Jason and Mandy were both so excited that their constant chatter and questions kept both Meagan and Adam occupied.

"Why is the capitol in Salem?" Jason wanted to know.

"I'm not sure," replied Meagan.

"It wasn't always, Jason. There was a time when the capital of Oregon was Oregon City. As to why they made the change, maybe there will be something on that at the Capitol Building." Adam sounded like the professor he was and Meagan hid a smile.

"How long until we get there?" demanded Mandy.

Adam rolled his eyes and Meagan laughed.

"It won't be for at least another half an hour," Adam replied.

"How long is a half an hour?"

"Thirty minutes."

"How long is that?"

"Long enough." Adam's short reply caused Meagan's laughter to overflow. He turned reproachful eyes on her.

She defended herself. "I can't help it."

"What's so amusing about my daughter asking more questions than a final exam before we are even on the freeway?"

She couldn't resist teasing him. "Maybe you should have Mandy write your final exams."

"Right. Whenever I'm stumped for a question, I can just ask my six-year-old daughter. Do you think my students will wonder why I want to know how long thirty minutes is?"

"Perhaps, but considering what you teach, they will likely answer 1,800 seconds."

"Undoubtedly thanking me for the easy points."

"Undoubtedly." It struck her that Adam was probably one of those professors she had avoided in college, the kind that gave such difficult tests only half of the class passed. "Are you a tough teacher, Adam?"

He turned his eyes briefly from the road and looked at her, apparently giving her question some serious thought. "I guess some would say that I am. I don't try to trick my students, though. If they know their stuff, they do well on my tests."

"Let me guess, about half of your students know their stuff. Am I right?"

"A few years ago, you might have been. That was before Caroline insisted on trying to take one of my final exams. A parent of one of my students worked with her and complained I was too hard on their child."

"Caroline wanted to prove how fair you were?"

Adam's face was unreadable. "Not exactly."

"What happened?"

"I gave her a Level 1 Algebra final. She got 36%."

"She must have been furious."

"That's putting it mildly."

"What did you do?"

"I looked over my test to see if it was really as difficult as everyone thought it was."

"Well, was it?" She knew the answer, but wanted to hear him admit it.

"Yes. After that, I asked my students for their input and developed a much better system of testing. However, it isn't easy. They still have to know their stuff."

"I bet."

He looked sideways at her. She returned his gaze with what she hoped was an innocent look.

"Just what is that supposed to mean?"

"I was only agreeing with you."

"Confess. You think I'm too hard on my students, don't you?"

She could hear the real concern in his voice. The conversation had become a code for something else: an exploration of their different approaches to life. Her accusations about him running a boot camp for Jason and Mandy came to mind.

"No, of course not, Adam. It's just that..." She couldn't finish her sentence. How could she say what was on her mind without sparking another argument and destroying their peaceful camaraderie?

"Just what?" He wasn't going to give up.

Now would be the time for an interruption from the backseat. No such luck. Both Jason and Mandy had been lulled to sleep by the movement of the car. "You're so...so regimented."

"Maybe that's why Caroline and I got along so well. Her career required a certain type of regimentation. I liked that aspect of it."

"How did you and Caroline meet?"

"We went to undergraduate school together. I met her in Physics. We started dating and fell in love. She accepted my proposal of marriage before she went into the military to finish her medical education."

"Oh, that explains it."

"Explains what?"

"How you ended up married to a career military wife. With your focus on stability, it's hard to see you choosing to marry someone whose career required frequent moves. However, love explains a lot."

She thought about her choice to marry Brian, a salesman who often had to travel out of town on business. It certainly wasn't a lifestyle she would have chosen, but because she loved him she never asked him to give it up. Perhaps she should have. Then maybe he and his secretary wouldn't have had the time and opportunity to make a baby.

Shaking off the depressing thoughts, she noticed that Adam looked like he was having some pretty negative thoughts of his own. If he gripped the steering wheel any harder, it would crack.

She put her hand on his arm. "I'm sorry. I didn't mean to bring up painful memories."

He relaxed his grip on the wheel, but his expression didn't change. "I didn't want Caroline to stay in the military after

Jason was born. That was our original plan. Caroline only entered the military to pay for her medical education. She could have found a permanent position in the private sector easily, but she didn't want to."

"She must have liked her job."

"Yes and she liked moving. She wanted to see other places, experience them. When she had Mandy and still insisted on re-enlisting, I gave up."

Meagan could feel his pain. He had good reason to want stability, considering his own childhood. He must have felt betrayed when Caroline changed her mind about getting out of the military. Meagan understood betrayal. It was a wound that didn't heal. An irresistible urge to smooth the unhappy lines from his face washed over her. Placing her hand on his shoulder, she squeezed.

The tense posture of his body relaxed. "Caroline was a good wife. We grew apart as we grew up. The two college students who fell in love became completely different people with divergent goals. Instead of becoming one, we became more individual. Still, we had a better marriage than most people I know."

"Yes. I can believe that. There are worse things than being married to a stranger."

Meagan thought about being married to someone you trusted and loved, but who betrayed everything you believed in. She and Brian hadn't disagreed about how they wanted to live. In fact, they had total agreement about what they wanted to do after the children came. Only no children came and Brian eventually gave up trying to share the dream with her.

Mandy and Jason's voices raised in argument interrupted her thoughts. They were awake and they were cranky. She turned her head to see what the problem was. "What's up, guys?"

"Jason watched a soap opera and now he says he didn't."

Jason looked guiltily at Meagan. "Did not."

Adam said, "Jason, if you did, it would be much better to tell the truth. Once a person loses the trust of the people who care for him, he has a hard time gaining it back."

"Yes, sir."

"Well, did you or didn't you?"

"I did." Jason's voice sounded sullen.

"Daddy, what's amnesia? Somebody on the show had it and it made her act strange, like she didn't know her own kids."

"You watched the show too, Mandy?" The tone of Adam's voice suggested she not hedge about it.

"Yes, Daddy, but what's amnesia?" Her attempt to change the subject went unheeded.

"I don't want either of you children watching shows like that. Do you understand?"

"Yes, Daddy."

"I understand, Dad."

"Are we there yet?" asked Mandy.

"Almost, this is our exit."

Four hours later, Meagan was convinced that Adam and Patty had gone to the same school for overzealous tour guides. After two hours at Gilbert House Children's Museum, they had gone to the Mission Mill. Adam had finally agreed to stop for lunch when Meagan and the children refused to enter the Capitol Building without refueling.

Meagan sat on the picnic blanket watching Jason and Mandy play. She turned her gaze toward Adam sitting next to her and caught him watching her. He was looking at her as if he could see into her very soul.

The silence between them became oppressive. Meagan said the first thing that came to her mind. "This is wonderful." She waved her arms indicating the park, the picnic basket and the children playing.

"Yes it is. I decided you were right about enjoying summer. Next year the children will be in school full-time. They deserve a little break."

"Are you sure you want to put them in school?"

He gave her a look that said she'd lost her marbles. "I've already explained all that."

"Explain it to me again."

Adam moved restlessly on the blanket, putting the last of the picnic lunch away in the basket. "I want Jason and Mandy to have the stability of a regular school schedule."

"What's the matter with the one they have now?"

"Meagan, homeschooling was the best alternative for them when we had to move every couple of years. Now that we're settled, or close to it, I think they need the constancy of seeing the same children every day and having the same teacher all year."

Meagan wondered what he meant by saying they were close to settled. Did it have something to do with the position he had interviewed for in Chicago? He hadn't brought it up in the month she had been there. She assumed he hadn't gotten it. "I've changed nannies six times since Caroline died. The children need more uniformity than that."

"I have no intention of going anywhere."

"Neither did any of their other nannies."

He couldn't make himself any clearer than that. Adam saw her as his nanny and nothing else. He was already making plans for when she left to minimize the trauma to his children.

"Besides, for you to homeschool them during the school year you'd have to be certified."

She picked up a stray plastic cup and deposited it in the basket. "I don't understand. I'm sure all of the homeschoolers in the group at church aren't certified teachers."

"They are parents. A parent doesn't have to be certified, but to have someone else teach your children is a different matter in the state of Oregon. I learned this the hard way when I hired my first nanny."

She felt a little better. She couldn't legally teach the children and Adam had no intention of finding a different nanny who could. The sudden thought that if the children were going to be at school during the day then they wouldn't need a nanny slammed into Meagan like a linebacker looking for the goal.

"How much longer?"

He stared at her, uncomprehending. "How much longer until what?"

"Until school starts, until you don't need a nanny anymore?"

"That's not going to happen. As a matter of fact, I wanted to talk to you about your schedule."

She grimaced. Adam and his schedules. "Why doesn't that surprise me? Has anyone ever told you that schedules might be too big a part of your life?"

He grinned. "Never. How about you? Anyone ever told you that you could stand to be a little more scheduled?"

She tilted her head, pretending to think about it. Shaking her head she said, "Never."

He laughed and the sound washed over her, calming her fear that he was planning to dismiss her in the fall. Surely he wouldn't be flirting if he was going to break the news that her job was almost over. Closing the picnic basket, Adam turned back to face her.

"About the schedule," said Adam.

"Yes?"

"Estelle wants to cut back to mornings so that she can spend more time with her daughter and grandchild. I'm hoping that you'll be willing to reverse your hours and be responsible for Jason and Mandy in the afternoons."

He wasn't planning on getting rid of her. Her heart started to beat again. "I think that could be arranged."

"I don't suppose you would take on the duty of preparing dinner as well?" He looked so hopeful; Meagan had serious doubts about her ability to say no. "I'm a lousy cook. Besides then you'll have all day to write."

He really was pulling out all of the stops. Shifting on the blanket so that both Mandy and Jason were in her line of vision, she nodded. "But I'm still not sure this private school idea is the way to go."

He reached out and gently massaged her arm. "It's going to be okay, Meagan. Jason and Mandy will settle in just fine at school."

How could he be so sure? "They're over a year ahead of other children their age academically. Do you think it will be good for Jason and Mandy to put them in a classroom of children all older than they are?"

He stood up with the basket in his hands. "I thought I would put them in their proper grades."

"They'll be bored to tears. They are both so bright, it will be like putting them in pre-school again."

"Surely it's not that drastic." His mocking tone irritated her.

"Close enough."

"No doubt it's better to do it now than to wait until the academic differences between the grades is more severe."

She knew he was right, but she didn't have to like it. She stood up and moved to where the children were playing. Soon she was pushing Mandy on the swing and cheering Jason on as he climbed a knotted rope to the top of the play structure.

Meagan turned her head to see Adam folding the blanket. He took it and the hamper to the car. She allowed Jason and Mandy to convince her to teeter-totter with them. They both leaned back, effectively trapping her aloft. She gave them a mock glare and demanded that they let her down.

Suddenly she felt her side being pulled down. Adam spoke into her ear as he drew her level. "It looks like you could use a little help."

"Dad! No fair. You're too big."

His hands were centimeters from her backside. The feelings she had experienced earlier at his closeness came rushing back. Jason and Mandy jumped off and she would have gone crashing to the ground if Adam had not been there.

"Those little hooligans. I could have been in the dirt."

"It's a good thing I came when I did." His smile was lethal.

"Yes. Thank you, kind sir." Her words ended in a squeak as Adam put his arm around her waist and lifted her off of the play equipment.

He didn't let her go immediately. Instead, he rubbed his cheek lightly against her hair. "I like the way you smell."

"What are you doing?" She wanted to sound outraged, but her voice came out ragged and breathy instead.

"I'm not sure, but it feels good, doesn't it?"

Was this Adam talking?

"Daddy's hugging Miss Meagan," shouted Mandy, loud enough for everyone at the park to hear.

Meagan squirmed with embarrassment.

"Should we give her something really good to shout about?" His voice held a teasing, husky quality that Meagan found entrancing. It took all of her inner reserve to pull herself from his arms.

"No."

"Coward."

Was she a coward? It felt odd to have Adam accusing her of a timid spirit. She was the adventuresome one. He was the stodgy professor. At least, that's what she thought. What was his game today? Was he seriously interested in deepening their relationship or was it the unreality of being away from home and their responsibilities?

Her thoughts wouldn't let her rest as she followed Adam into the Capitol Rotunda.

"Can we go up to the dome?" asked Jason.

"I don't think so, buddy," replied Adam.

"But a kid in church said he and his class did."

"I'm sure they got special permission."

"Can't we get permission?" asked Mandy.

Meagan could see that both Jason and Mandy had their hearts set on seeing the dome. "We can try."

"I doubt it," said Adam.

"Now who's the coward?"

Adam smiled at her rejoinder. "Fine, let's find someone and ask."

"Cool," Jason said as he high-fived his sister.

Adam walked to the information desk to ask. Meagan found herself praying that the children wouldn't be disappointed. A foolish prayer for a woman afraid of heights.

Adam returned. "They're taking a tour up now. If we hurry, we can join them."

Meagan's heart fluttered. "I'll just stay down here and wait for you."

"But Miss Meagan. You have to come," said Jason.

"Yeah, it won't be any fun without you," cajoled Mandy.

How bad could it be? She would just have to strengthen her weak knees and go for it. "Okay. I'll go."

80

"Isn't this great? Look down there, Dad. Doesn't it look cool?"

His son's voice filled with awed enthusiasm resounded in his heart like a joyful crescendo. Adam moved to stand by Meagan at the rail, wanting to share this moment with her. "I'm glad you talked me into asking if we could come up. The view up here is incredible."

Meagan didn't answer.

Mandy tugged on Meagan's T-shirt. "Miss Meagan, please lift me up. I can't see."

"Come here, squirt, I'll lift you up." Adam reached for his daughter, but she avoided his hands.

"Daddy, I think something's wrong with Miss Meagan. She looks strange."

Adam moved so that he could see Meagan's face. Strange? She looked terrified. Her knuckles were white where she gripped the rail and her eyes had the unfocused gaze of someone in the grip of paralyzing fear. "Don't look down. Turn your head and look at me." He placed his hand against the silky softness of her hair and gently forced her to look away from the view. "That's right."

She looked into his eyes and her pupils slowly came back into focus. He continued prying her fingers away from the rail one by one. When he succeeded he turned her body toward his, hugging her tightly against himself. Eventually the tremors that shook her body stilled.

"I really am a coward." Her voice was thick with tears.

"Don't cry, honey. You're not a coward. I wish you had told me you're acrophobic."

She hiccupped as she laughed through her tears. "Adam, you even sound like a professor when you're comforting me."

If she felt good enough to tease him, she was definitely doing better. He sighed with relief. "What do you expect? I *am* a professor."

The tour guide came over. "Is she all right?"

Meagan nodded against his chest and tried to pull away. He reluctantly allowed her to step back.

"She'll be fine."

"Don't be embarrassed, ma'am. You're not the first person to react this way to the view." Adam appreciated the man's attempt to diminish Meagan's discomfort.

"I think I'll go down now."

Adam agreed. "Jason, Mandy, time to go."

Meagan's head snapped up. "I didn't mean for you all to leave. I don't want to spoil your fun."

Adam barely resisted the urge to laugh. She didn't know it, but she looked as forlorn as if she had just lost her pet kitten. He had no intention of letting her navigate the stairs alone. The look of terror on her face when she was looking over the railing had stirred up a strong urge to protect. "Don't worry. You aren't spoiling our fun. Now, let's go troops."

He took her arm to lead her down the stairs and the children followed close behind.

"Remember to hold the rail walking down the stairs."

Even in her distress, she was trying to care for his children. Warmth unfurled in his heart.

When they emerged from the stairwell, she tried to pull away. He wouldn't let go. He was glad that she wasn't immune to his touch. He didn't want to suffer alone, especially in this. He led her and the children to the car. It was time to go home.

"Thank you, Adam." Her voice was low as if she didn't want the children to hear.

"You're welcome, but why?"

She looked at him as if she couldn't believe he didn't know what she was talking about. He didn't though. He hoped she would explain. Her mind worked in ways he didn't understand.

"You didn't berate me for being afraid. Brian used to tell me to get a grip on myself and expect me to be fine."

"I'm not Brian."

"No, you are not."

The way she said it made him feel like it was a compliment. She seemed so vulnerable right now, he hated the thought that anyone had belittled her fears.

"I know I was stupid to go with you, but I didn't want to disappoint the children. Thanks for rescuing me."

"No problem, any time." He meant it. He wanted to be around to rescue her whenever she needed it.

After an uneventful journey home, he pulled into the gravel drive in front of the farmhouse. Jason and Mandy had both fallen asleep. Adam parked the car and turned to Meagan. She was awake.

"I thought you fell asleep."

She shook her head, but didn't speak.

"Well, I'm glad. I think carrying you to bed would have been my downfall."

That got a response. "Adam!"

"Shh, you'll wake the children." He smiled at her wide-eyed stare. A speechless Meagan was a rarity.

"I'll take Jason up if you don't mind waiting here in the car with Mandy." Not waiting for a response, he got out of the car. He went around to the back and lifted Jason out of his seat belt.

Adam came out of Jason's room just as Meagan reached the top of the stairs. She was carrying Mandy. Leading the way to Mandy's room, he stepped aside after opening the door for Meagan. They made short work of preparing his daughter for bed. Images of the first night she had stayed with them came to his mind. He had been irritated with her for keeping his children up past their bedtime. This time it had been his idea and he didn't feel guilty, not at all.

They moved into the hallway. Meagan eyed her door. He knew she wanted to escape to her room. She hadn't fooled him pretending to be asleep on the drive home. She was scared of the feelings between them. So was he, but he wasn't willing to ignore it any longer.

He stepped closer to Meagan, backing her against the wall. "Good night."

She stood, completely still, like a doe in a clearing that scents danger, but doesn't know what direction it's coming from. She tried to put distance between them with words. "Good night, Adam, and thank you. Today was a lovely day."

He moved closer. "Yes, it was."

His lips were inches from hers and he desperately wanted to close the gap. He needed some sign from her that it was okay to do so. She licked her lips nervously and he brushed his finger lightly where her tongue had been.

He placed his arms around her gently, hoping she wouldn't pull away, but knowing if she did that he would let her go. She came toward him, her head tilted slightly toward his own.

"Meagan?"

He slid his hand into her hair and pulled her face until only a breath separated their lips.

He repeated her name. Her eyes, which had almost closed, opened. Finally, he thought she understood what he was asking.

"Yes. Adam. Yes, please."

His mouth settled on hers in a tender caress.

Chapter Eight

As Adam pulled her to him, Meagan sighed in surrender to the kiss. This is what she had desired all day, but had been too afraid to hope for.

She wanted to hold him like this forever with his lips moving gently over hers, coaxing her to respond. She parted hers and heard him groan as he hungrily deepened the kiss. His hands were caressing her back and pulling her body so close that she felt molded to him. It was a wonderful sensation. Coherent thought became impossible.

Sanity returned however and she pushed gently from his arms. "Please, Adam, we should stop."

He resisted the pressure of her hands against his chest at first, but at her words his eyes opened and he stepped away from her. His breathing was ragged and she could see a rapid pulse in his neck. She felt feminine satisfaction that Adam was every bit as overwhelmed as she was by the kiss.

"You're right. We should." He took a deep breath, expelling it slowly. "I forgot how mind-blowing a simple kiss could be."

Simple kiss? Not for her, it hadn't been.

Meagan moved backward, intending to escape to her room. Adam's voice stopped her. "Then again, maybe I didn't forget, maybe it's just never been this good."

They were headed for deep waters and she wasn't sure she still remembered how to swim in them. She said, "See you in the morning," before slipping into her room and closing the door. For the longest time she leaned against it, allowing herself to relive the sensation of Adam's kiss.

Pushing away from the door, Meagan readied herself for bed. She stopped often, just to stare into space. It was embarrassing to be so affected by a kiss. She had been married. She knew the pleasure of much deeper intimacy and yet something about Adam's kiss affected her in a way that Brian's most intimate caresses had not.

Peeking out in the hallway, she saw that Adam's door was closed. She tiptoed to the bathroom to brush her teeth. Looking in the mirror, she took herself firmly in hand. *This is not the way a professional nanny behaves. You do not allow your employer to steal kisses late at night, or any other time for that matter.* The face that peered back at her was unrepentant. She looked well kissed and dreamy eyed.

This was not a good sign. If she and Adam had any kind of future together, she wanted to take the right steps to get there. Those steps did not include passionate kisses in the hallway. Kisses that might lead to more. They were too risky.

Because if she and Adam *didn't* have a future together, those kinds of kisses would lead only to regrets. She wasn't convinced a long-term relationship was even possible with him. Adam had loosened up, a little. She could probably get used to a tad more schedule in her life. Would it be enough? That was a question her tired brain did not have an answer for.

The only thing she did know was that Adam had kissed her. It did not follow that he was looking for a relationship and she needed to remember that. His comments earlier that day implied that he saw her position as his nanny in a more temporary light than she did, even if he didn't intend to let her go in the fall. The kiss probably meant nothing to him at all. He had as much as admitted that he hadn't expected it to carry such a punch.

Mind-blowing. She smiled to herself. Not bad.

ॐ

Adam sat at his desk looking over the job offer from the Illinois university. A sense of unreality surrounded him like a blanket, blocking the sound of the fan that forced air much too warm for early morning to circulate in the room. He also ignored the tempting plate of breakfast that sat on the side of his desk.

It had taken the hiring committee so long to get back to him, he had been convinced they had decided on another candidate. Now this. Shock was a mild word for the way he felt when the dean had called the previous morning to give him the word and informed him that an express package would be delivered later that day with the formal documents.

After a nearly incoherent conversation, he had hung up the phone and done something he never did. He cancelled his day at the university, asked Estelle to pack a picnic lunch and invited Meagan and the children to join him in his escape.

Unfortunately, the trip had only added to the complications surrounding his decision. Insanity was the only justification he could come up with for his actions the previous day. And it wasn't much of an excuse as excuses went. He had treated Meagan like a lover, not a nanny.

Then there was the kiss. If she had not broken it off, he was not sure when he would have. The temptation to take her straight to bed had been overwhelming. He wasn't proud of the

115

fact. He had asked God to forgive him for putting himself and Meagan in such a precarious position. Now he had to ask Meagan.

Pushing aside the job offer, he pulled out his Bible and opened to his favorite passage. Reading the words of Psalm 139 over again, he tried to let them settle in his heart. He needed peace and guidance.

Everything had seemed so clear before Meagan came. If he were offered the position, he would go to his dean and tell him that as much as he wanted to stay, he would leave in order to secure an endowed chair. He hoped it would be the impetus his dean needed to go to bat for him with the faculty board to grant him tenure. If it wasn't, he had been fully prepared to take the job offer and move to Illinois.

He was no longer convinced that was an option. If he wasn't willing to move, wouldn't it be sheer manipulation and even deceitful to imply that he might to gain his own ends?

Looking down at the job offer once again, he prayed for wisdom. He couldn't get the image of Meagan's face from his mind. *Lord, are you telling me I should talk to Meagan about this? You know how she's going to respond. For a free-spirited person, she doesn't react well to change. Look at how she argued with me about putting Jason and Mandy in private school and that was after she as good as told me that schooling them in the summer was no better than boot camp.*

Hearing three sharp raps on his study door, Adam called, "Come in."

Meagan stood in the door, looking as confused and uncertain as he felt. "Adam, I, um, I was praying and I had this strong feeling that you and I need to talk. I'd rather just ignore it, but I guess we have to deal with last night sooner or later."

He didn't laugh because of sheer willpower. *I get the picture, Lord.* He stood up and moved around the desk. She had not ventured any farther into the room than the doorway. "Let's go for a walk." He didn't want Jason or Mandy to accidentally overhear the conversation.

"Fine."

"Wait here." When she nodded her acquiescence, he went to the kitchen to ask Estelle to make sure the children had their breakfast and watch over them until he and Meagan returned.

He went back to Meagan and taking her arm, he led her out the front door. They walked down the long driveway in silence, the only sound the crunch of gravel under their feet and early morning birdsong.

"I owe you an apology." The stark words were not what he had meant to say, but they would do.

She stumbled. Tightening his grip on her arm, he steadied her. She yanked her arm away from him and came close to tripping again. "What did you say?"

"I said, I was sorry."

"That's what I thought." The words came out an accusation. She was rapidly putting distance between them. If she went any farther, she would be walking in the road. "Before I forgive you, maybe you should tell me just exactly what you are sorry for."

Something had gone wrong. She was furious. He deserved her wrath for taking advantage of her tired state the previous evening and forcing her to call a halt to their kiss, but for the life of him he couldn't figure out why she was angry now. He was trying to make it right.

"I'm sorry that I took advantage of you last night."

Her snort of annoyance told him he was far from making it better. "I'm a grown woman. All you did was kiss me. I'm not about to cry foul and demand a marriage proposal."

"I know that. Look, I'm sorry that I didn't keep my libido under control. If you hadn't pulled away, I don't know how far I would have gone." He hated admitting it to her. It had been hard enough admitting the truth to the Lord.

She stopped her fast moving feet and turned her head to face him. "You're not sorry you kissed me?"

Where did this woman get her ideas? The working of her mind was a complete mystery to him sometimes. "No."

She moved off the road to walk beside him again. "You're just sorry you didn't know when to quit?"

Did she have to rub it in? "Yes."

Placing her hand on his arm, she smiled brilliantly at him. "You are forgiven."

He couldn't help grinning back. Her hand on his arm felt right. "Thank you."

"You're welcome." He almost kissed the cheeky grin right off her face. The fact that they were walking on a very public road in view of one of his nosiest neighbors was all that stopped him.

Gripping her hand, he continued walking and savored the feel of her body so close to his. As they approached the opening to a path in the forest, he pulled her toward it. "There was something else I wanted to talk to you about."

Inclining her head, she looked at him. "What is it?"

"The dean from Illinois called yesterday."

She stiffened next to him, her fingers curling tightly around his. "What did he say?"

"He offered me the job."

She stopped walking again and gave him an accusing glare. "You aren't going to take it, are you?"

You see, Lord. I told you she'd react this way. "It's not that easy."

"Of course it is. All you have to do is say you've changed your mind and you don't want to move."

"It's not that simple." He told her about his initial reasons for interviewing and the quandary he was in now.

"You're saying that you would have moved before?" She sounded appalled. "Jason and Mandy love their life on the farm. How could you move them? They are happy here. They are *secure.*"

He brushed a stray curl behind her ear. "I know. But part of their security lies in my employment." He wanted her to understand. He was trying to do what was best for his children.

She pulled her hand from his and paced on the forest path in her agitation. "You told me that your classes always have waiting lists. They aren't going to fire you, Adam." Stopping her pacing, she fixed him with a look filled with censure.

"Tenure or an endowed chair would give *me* more security. It would let me rest easier at night."

"But, Adam, your security doesn't rest in your job. It rests in Christ. He's your surety, the Rock on which you can stand." She came close and gripped his upper arms, punctuating her words with tiny shakes.

Her proximity made it hard to keep his focus on their discussion. All he wanted to do was reach out and pull her the remaining ten inches for her body to rest against his. "I know that, but I still have a responsibility to make sound career decisions."

"You think it would be a sound decision to uproot your children and move them half way across the country?" The outrage in her voice left him in no doubt of how she felt about his possible career plans.

"That's not why I interviewed. I wanted leverage for my current position."

She crossed her arms over her chest and stepped back. "Well, you have it. They offered you the job."

He didn't want to explain it again, but he had to. "That's not the problem. The problem is that I'm not sure I'd be willing to take the job."

"You were sure before?"

He sighed. This was the sticky part. "Yes."

"What changed?"

Meagan's earlier pacing had taken them deeper into the forest. They were now surrounded by a shelter of trees, shielded from the view of his neighbors. He wished that he was as well hidden from Meagan. He definitely did not want to answer that question.

She tapped her foot against the forest path. "I asked what changed."

"You and the way you make me see life differently than I ever have." He hoped she was satisfied. He might as well have shouted his growing feelings from the rooftop. She would probably gloat. He had already admitted that he didn't have complete control of his physical response to her.

She didn't gloat. She just stood there, silent and watchful. "I don't understand. Are you saying that you aren't sure that you want to move because I made you see that Jason and Mandy need more fun in their life?"

"That's part of it. You have become an important person to my children and I don't want them to lose you."

"What is the other part?"

A terrier had nothing on tenacity when it came to Meagan. "The other part is that I'm not sure I want to lose you."

ༀ

"You're zoning off again."

Meagan turned to Patty, reining in her wayward thoughts. She tried to focus on her friend and the scenery out the car window, anything but Adam. It had been three days since her discussion in the woods with Adam. She had already spent too much of those three days contemplating his admission that he didn't want to lose her, or to be perfectly correct that he wasn't sure he wanted to lose her. That was the crux of her disjointed thoughts. He admitted to feelings for her, but was obviously uncertain about their extent and whether or not he even wanted them.

"I'm sorry, Patty. What were you saying?"

"I asked if there was anything on your mind. You've been off in La-La Land since you arrived at the church."

Meagan looked behind her to the ten children occupying the other seats of the church's van. She wasn't about to spill her guts to Patty with ten extra sets of ears hanging on her every word.

"Don't worry about them. I know from past experience that if you're sitting in the passenger seats of this van you can't hear a blessed thing from the front. I've tried to carry on a conversation with the driver from the back before, but had to give up." Patty's assurance of privacy was boosted by the sound of *Kids Praise* blasting from the rear speakers.

Meagan toyed with the strap of her purse, unsure what she wanted to tell Patty. She couldn't say anything about Adam's job offer without breaking his confidence. "Did you know that Adam took the day off to escort the children and me on a day trip?"

Patty smiled beatifically at another driver making unkind hand gestures at her for going the speed limit in the middle lane. "I didn't know that, but I'm not surprised considering the other things he's been doing out of character lately."

Meagan was intrigued. "What do you mean?"

"Well, there's the small discrepancy of you all attending the late service at church twice this month."

"Oh, that. He couldn't expect the children to get up early after movie night."

Patty chuckled. "According to Mandy, movie night is your invention. Before you came, Adam was religious about their bedtime."

Meagan waved her hand. "He just needed to loosen up a little. He enjoys movie night every bit as much as the children do." She didn't mention that Adam seemed to enjoy watching her react to the movies more than he liked the shows themselves. He laughed at her emotional displays, often pointing out that it was "just a movie".

Patty nodded. "I couldn't agree more. Adam's a very nice man, but he's too regimented. At any rate, the fact that you convinced him to allow Jason and Mandy to accompany us today is nothing short of phenomenal."

"He's not that bad about his schedule. He understood me wanting to take them on a field trip. It really wasn't all that hard."

Patty signaled to exit to go downtown. "Meagan, you did tell Adam where we're going today didn't you?"

Preoccupied by a car that insisted on cutting in front of the van at the exit, Meagan responded inattentively. "We talked about it the other day in his study."

Forced to concentrate on navigating the heavy traffic of downtown Portland, Patty didn't answer. When they arrived at the homeless shelter, she gave a short lecture to the children on safety and sticking together. Meagan talked to them about treating the people they met that day with respect and the love of Jesus. Confident that the children would abide by the rules, the women led them into the homeless shelter.

The director, a young woman wearing a T-shirt and jeans, greeted them. "Hello." She turned to Patty. "I see that you've brought me a small army of helpers today."

Patty beamed at her. "You bet. They're ready and willing to work."

"Great. Friday is one of our busiest days and we'll need extra hands serving the food and cleaning the tables. Think your crew can handle it?"

"Of course they can. Our kids want to do what they can to share the love of Jesus with others." Jake's voice boomed from behind Meagan. She turned around to smile a greeting at him and the two boys that had ridden in his car.

"Terrific. Let's get to it then." The director began assigning tasks. She assigned Meagan the chore of overseeing clean up of the tables. It wasn't an easy job. Not only did she have to make sure that empty plates and used cutlery made it to the garbage, she also had to oversee the three children helping her. They wanted to talk to the patrons of the shelter, which wasn't a problem until an obviously drunken man wanted to talk to Mandy.

"Come here, sweetie, you remind me of my sweet Marie." The man's rheumy eyes were filled with tears. "I lost my little girl."

Mandy stared at the man. "You mean you can't find her?"

The man shook his head sadly. "No. I lost her to the demon rum. Her ma couldn't stand it any more and she left me."

Mandy put her hand on the ragged sleeve of the man's shirt. "I'm sorry you lost your little girl. Maybe you should get rid of the demon rum. Demons are bad. The Bible says so."

The man started crying, his head bobbing up and down in agreement with Mandy's words. "You're right. You're right, but I can't fight the demon."

"But, sir, Jesus can fight him. Pastor Jake will pray for you if you want."

"Do you think he would?" The man sounded pathetically eager.

Meagan stepped forward. "Mandy, please go find Pastor Jake."

"Okay, Miss Meagan." Mandy walked away, intent on her quest to find Jake, and Meagan sighed with relief. She wanted the children to experience ministry first hand, but inebriated men were unreliable. The man could go from tearful self-pity to fury in seconds. Meagan had seen it in similar circumstances back in Scottsdale.

She turned back to the man, now rocking on his chair and muttering to himself. She picked up an empty plate from the vacated spot next to him and tossed it into her garbage bag. A woman, her face heavy with make-up and clothes that could have been painted on, immediately filled the empty spot.

"Hey, you part of the churchies helping serve today?" The woman's voice was as loud as her orange spiky hair.

"I guess you could call us that." Something about this scantily clad stranger struck a chord in Meagan. "My name is Meagan. What's yours?"

"They call me Baby."

"It's nice to meet you, Baby."

The other woman laughed. She responded with heavy sarcasm. "Oh, yeah, nice."

Meagan wasn't put off by Baby's mockery. "You know us 'churchies', we like meeting everybody."

"Yeah, I guess." She was silent while Meagan continued to clean. When Jake, having left Mandy to help in the kitchen, came over to pray for the man, Baby stopped eating. She watched Jake pray with a surprising intensity.

Jake finished praying and moved on to speak to someone else. The man got up and wandered out the door, no longer muttering about his lost Marie.

Acting on instinct, Meagan sat down next to Baby. "Would you like someone to pray with you?"

Baby looked up, startled. "Uh, I don't know. I'm not sure you can pray for someone like me."

"When it comes to prayer, there's no such thing as 'someone like me'. If you want me to pray, I'd be glad to."

"Maybe you don't know what I am."

Meagan laid her hand over the other woman's and squeezed. "You are Baby and God loves you."

"My name is Ruth. My street name is Baby."

"Ruth? That's a beautiful name. It comes from the Bible. Did you know that?"

Ruth shook her head.

"Ruth was an incredible woman who showed great loyalty and faith to her family and to God. She was one of Christ's ancestors. He had another ancestor you might be interested in. You and she have something in common."

"Who's that?" Ruth's voice vibrated with interest.

"Rahab. Rahab was another woman who showed faith. She was very courageous."

"Sounds like a pretty special lady. But we ain't got anything in common."

"You'd be surprised. Rahab was a prostitute and she had the courage to change her life."

"You said she was one of Christ's ancestors?"

"Yes."

"No way."

"Jesus himself said that he came to save the sinners and the lost."

"I guess it would be okay if you prayed for me."

Meagan did, pouring hope for Ruth into her words. Before Ruth left, Meagan asked her if there was a way that she could meet with her again. "I'd like to give you a Bible and you can read about Ruth and Rahab on your own."

Ruth gave her the address of a motel. "I just eat here, I don't live here. In my line of work, you've got to have a room."

Meagan nodded, making a mental note to stop by and visit the other woman as soon as possible. The rest of the time at the shelter went by quickly. Before she realized it, Jake was saying that it was time to go. She looked around the shelter with longing.

"I understand. It's hard to leave, isn't it? You meet these people that are in so much need and you hate to go back to your neatly ordered world."

Meagan sighed. "Exactly."

She and Patty didn't try to visit on the way back to the church. The children were too loud, singing along with *Kids Praise* and shouting back and forth. When they arrived at the church, everyone gathered in the sanctuary to pray for those they had ministered to that morning and afternoon. They also thanked God for his provision and ministering to them through the homeless shelter.

On the way home in the car, Jason and Mandy regaled Meagan with their impression of their hours at the shelter. Jason had served in the food line. "Mrs. Patty let me serve the mashed potatoes. It was fun. Everybody liked them, not like the vegetables. Some people swore about the vegetables. One guy even threatened Mrs. Patty if she put any on his plate."

"What did Mrs. Patty do?" asked Meagan.

"She told him to mind his manners."

That sounded like Patty.

"Are you two glad you went?"

Jason agreed with enthusiasm. "Yeah. I'm really glad. Dad wouldn't let us go last year and Jimmy Nelson met a guy with blue hair. Now I can tell him I met a guy with an earring in his nose."

"Jason, you did not go to the shelter to have something to boast about to Jimmy Nelson."

"Yes, Miss Meagan."

Several comments Patty had made clicked into place for Meagan. Dreading the answer, she asked, "Why wouldn't your father let you go last year?"

"He said he didn't want us exposed to those elements."

Mandy agreed. "Yeah, he wouldn't even talk about it to Mrs. Patty. He said no meant no. I'm glad he said yes to you Miss Meagan."

Had he said yes? What exactly had she *said* about today's activity? Meagan racked her brain trying to remember if she had actually told Adam where they were going. Recalling the conversation in his study, her heart sank.

Meagan pulled into the driveway, praying for a reprieve. She needed time to consider how she was going to explain herself to Adam. *Well, I guess I can recognize no when I hear it too, Lord.*

Not only was Adam's Volvo parked in front of the house, but Adam himself sat in a wicker chair on the front porch, drinking a glass of ice tea.

Jason and Mandy piled out of the car and ran up the steps. Adam stood up to hug them. "So, tell me about your field trip. What did you learn?"

Meagan looked around desperately for a place to hide.

Chapter Nine

Turning dazed eyes to his son, Adam asked, "You went where?"

In the stillness of the soft summer afternoon, his words sounded like a cannon shot to Meagan's oversensitive ears. She hesitated at the bottom of the porch steps. He had stood up when she parked her car and now he towered over her and the children like an avenging angel.

"To the shelter downtown," replied Jason, standing next to Adam.

Adam shook his head as if he couldn't take it in. He looked from Jason to Mandy and then at Meagan. She felt like a coward remaining on the walk and moved to drag her reluctant feet up the steps to the porch. Adam watched her like a lion with his prey. *Lord, remember Daniel? I could use a little help here, too.*

"Thanks for letting us go, Daddy. It was fun." Mandy's enthusiastic gratitude succeeded in gaining Adam's full attention.

He looked at his daughter as if she had sprouted two heads. "*I let you go?*" He turned his eyes back to Meagan and she couldn't mistake the slow simmer in his gaze. Adam was furious.

"Yeah, thanks for saying yes this year, Dad. It was great. I met this guy with an earring in his nose. Oh, and I got to serve the mashed potatoes."

Oh no, not now. They needed to talk about the ministry first. "Perhaps we could save the description of your duties until later." Meagan's voice sounded strangled, even to her own ears.

"I'd much rather hear it now."

Meagan flinched at Adam's tone of voice, but Jason appeared unfazed. "It was way more fun to give the homeless people food they liked. They used some words I never heard before about Mrs. Patty's vegetables."

Meagan wanted to crawl under the porch. Jason, in his innocence, was making the trip sound like a crash course in vulgarity.

"Did they?" How could anyone imbue so much disapproval into two little words?

"Yeah, but I didn't mind. Pastor Jake said that people use different words to express themselves."

Meagan groaned. Giving the boy a warning glance, she said, "I'm sure Jason would never repeat any of the words he heard today."

Jason didn't look convinced and neither did Adam. Ignoring Meagan's attempt to placate him, Adam turned to his daughter and asked what she had learned at the shelter.

"It was really great, Daddy. I got to work cleaning in the dining room, but after the man told me I was like his lost little girl I worked in the kitchen."

Meagan moaned inwardly. Why were the most interesting experiences also the ones that sounded the worst?

"What man?" Adam's voice was deceptively mild. The fire in his eyes convinced Meagan that he was anything but calm.

She tried to forestall further anger on his part. "It sounds much worse than it was."

He didn't even favor her with a glance. "Mandy, tell me about the man."

"He was so sad, Daddy. I asked Pastor Jake to pray for him because he had a demon. Its name was Rum. Have you ever heard of a demon named Rum?"

Emotions kaleidoscoped across Adam's face. Meagan saw confusion followed by pain and finally the banked fury returned. He needed to understand. This wasn't about exposing his children to unsavory elements. It was about ministry. "The important thing is that the man allowed Jake to pray for him."

Adam finally looked at her. Meagan fleetingly wished he hadn't. His eyes were filled with accusation that hit her with the force of a blow. "On the contrary, the important thing is that my daughter and son have been exposed to a side of life I've worked very hard to leave behind."

Jason looked back and forth between Meagan and Adam, his face filled with boyish concern. "But Dad, you told Miss Meagan we could go."

Meagan hated the look of sad reproach in Adam's eyes. He thought she had lied to his children. "You did. Give me permission that is."

She watched as Adam slumped back in his chair and he passed his hand across his eyes. When he spoke, his voice was filled with overwhelming fatigue. "Whatever you say, Meagan. Could we table this discussion until later?"

She heard the unspoken addendum, until they were alone. She nodded and headed inside. Once she arrived in her room, she closed and locked her door. A confusion of feelings rushing through her, she collapsed on the bed.

This was unbelievable. Adam thought she had lied to Jason and Mandy. How could he think something so vile about her? She would never lie to his children. Never.

She leaped up from the bed and began pacing in the confines of her room. Dashing away a stray tear with the back of her hand, she furiously listed off the reasons why Adam should trust her.

She loved Jason and Mandy. Hadn't she proven that by moving away from her family and friends to take care of them? Wasn't it obvious to Adam that she cared more deeply for his children than the average nanny?

She *was* trustworthy. She'd proven that by homeschooling Jason and Mandy when she thought it was a ridiculous schedule to keep in the summer. She could have gotten out of it several days a week. She was resourceful, but she hadn't. Adam could trust her, darn it.

Besides, she loved him.

The realization was like a bomb exploding in her brain. Stumbling to the chair at her desk, she sat down with a thump. Suddenly the room took on a clarity it had not had before. The colors on her quilt seemed brighter. Her hands grasped tightly in her lap came into sharp focus.

She loved Adam McCallister, overzealous schedules and all.

Insight into her love for Adam brought on fresh waves of desolation. Adam didn't love her. He couldn't and still believe that she would lie to his children. He wasn't even sure he cared if he lost her. Strike that, he was probably sure now that he *didn't* care. He would take the job in Illinois and leave her behind without a backward glance.

Why hadn't she told him where they were going? It was all so stupid. She had just assumed that since Patty and Jake were involved it was okay. That was what Adam had told her the first time she agreed to stay with the children.

Righteous indignation filled her. This was not her fault. It was Adam's and she'd be bushwhacked if she was going to allow the man she loved to mistrust her because of his own unclear directions.

Rising from the chair, Meagan was determined to find Adam and make him see the truth. He was going to apologize and that was that. Then maybe, just maybe, he'd tell her he was *sure* he didn't want to lose her.

ॐ

Adam felt unbearable pressure building inside. If he didn't get away, he was going to shout at someone. After asking Estelle to keep an eye on the children, he took off across the fields. He headed toward the forest that separated his farm from the one behind him. He needed to be alone to think.

The soft breeze that caressed his skin was in contrast with the harsh emotions that warred in his chest. He couldn't believe the day was the same as yesterday, full of sun-drenched flowers and warm blue skies. It should be raining and the wind should be howling like the storm brewing inside of him.

It shocked him that Meagan's betrayal hurt so much. He felt empty inside, like he had lost his wife all over again. But that was ridiculous. Meagan was his nanny. An attractive one, but his nanny nonetheless. She was not his wife or even close to it.

Who was he trying to kid? The feelings he had for Meagan went beyond anything an employer felt for his employee. How could she have lied to his children and gone behind his back to take Mandy and Jason to the homeless shelter? Surely Patty had told her how he felt about this particular Friendship Club excursion. He had made his feelings very clear the year before when Patty had asked if Jason could accompany them.

He bent down and picked up a rock and furiously threw it at a tree. It smacked against the bark and fell back to the ground. The action did nothing to dispel the frustration coursing through him. He kept walking, taking long brisk strides, storming over fallen logs and other obstructions in his path. He wasn't going back to the house until he had his anger under control. He didn't want the children to witness him fighting with Meagan.

He remembered the shouting matches from his childhood. His mother yelling at his father, demanding he change. His father yelling back, then breaking down and pleading for forgiveness. But the lies had never ended. The forgiveness had just led to more pain, more disenchantment, more lies.

He didn't blame his mother for forgiving, but why had she stayed? Why had she continued to believe a raving alcoholic? His father always had some excuse, some reason he was forced to lie, forced to let them down. His mother chose to believe.

Adam wasn't that stupid.

If Meagan had lied to the children and gone behind his back, she couldn't stay. There was no more room in his life for betrayal. His tolerance in that area was used up by the time he turned twelve.

Meagan's stricken face floated before his mind's eye. There was the slim possibility that today's trip was the result of a misunderstanding. She claimed he had given her permission. Perhaps she truly believed he had.

The thought did not settle the turmoil in his heart. His marriage to Caroline had left scars every bit as deep as his father's addiction. He had thought they were two halves of the same whole, only to discover that their views on family life were more like the North and South Pole—separated by distance and direction.

Regardless of whether or not Meagan had schemed and lied, her opinions on child rearing and family were as far from his as Caroline's had been. He needed to accept that now. He had tried to believe that he could compromise with Meagan. He even acknowledged that some of her techniques and ideas brought out the best in his children. This could not compensate for the fact that she was willing to put ministry above Jason and Mandy's safety and well-being.

After a childhood filled with pain, there was no way he was going to allow anyone, even a gorgeous redhead with a tender heart, to expose his daughter and son to that side of life. They were too young. They deserved a childhood unmarred by other people's addictions and hopelessness.

His anger spent, Adam headed back to the house. It was time to talk to Meagan.

He found her pacing his study. Walking inside, he pulled the door shut behind him. She whipped around to face him at the soft click of the tumbler falling into place.

"It's about time you got back."

Skirting her agitated form, he took a seat behind his desk. "I needed some time to think."

"About how I lied to your children?" Her scathing tone left him in no doubt about her feelings. While he had been cooling his anger, Meagan had been nursing hers.

The last thing he wanted was a full-blown argument. "Among other things." He indicated a chair. "Would you like to sit down?"

Folding her arms across her chest and bracing her legs apart, she glared at him. "I'd rather stand."

She wasn't going to make this easy. "Suit yourself."

"Well?" She sounded like a field marshal.

"Well, what?"

"Don't play games with me, Adam. You think I lied to Jason and Mandy about having your permission to go to the homeless shelter."

"Did you?"

"No. But I don't expect you to believe me."

"Then why are we having this conversation?"

Suddenly the fight went out of her and she sank into a chair in front of his desk. "Because I want you to."

"You want me to believe you?"

"Yes."

"Okay, explain to me how I gave you permission to do something I would never allow my children to do."

She took exception to his wording. He could see that right away. She bolted upright in her chair and her lovely chin jutted straight out. "Did you or did you not tell me that any excursion that Patty and Jake approved of would be fine by you?"

He racked his brain, trying to remember saying such a thing. Finally, he gave up. "When did I say that?"

"When I asked if you wanted me to go over the list of tourist attractions I wanted to visit while you were in Illinois."

Recognition dawned. "Meagan, that was about tourist attractions. The homeless shelter is not a tourist attraction."

She cast him a disgruntled look. "I know that."

"Then how could you construe that as permission to go?"

"When I told you about the field trip with the Friendship Club, you didn't ask where we were going."

She wasn't going to succeed in tossing the blame back on him. "And you didn't think it was important to tell me you wanted to take my children downtown to a homeless shelter?"

She jumped up from her chair and leaned over his desk. Her next words came out in a near shout. "Obviously not. I didn't tell you, did I?"

He wasn't going to give in. Leaning forward, he used a technique that worked very well with his children. He spoke quietly. "No. You did not."

She threw her hands in the air. "It was a mistake. What do you want me to say? I'm sorry. I won't do it again."

"That's a start."

She exploded. "Adam McCallister, sometimes you make me mad enough to scream. What on earth is wrong with Jason and Mandy experiencing more of life than the confines of this farm?"

He stood up to face her. "I don't want my children exposed to the same sordid mess I had to live through as a child."

"The shelter is not a sordid mess. It's full of individual people. Sure, some of them have addictions, but some of them don't. Some are families just like you and Jason and Mandy, but they've run out of options."

"I don't care. I'll give money to the shelter. I do that already, but I don't want my children down there."

"I already said I wouldn't do it again. What do you want from me, blood?"

Suddenly the study door burst open and Jason came careening into the room. "Stop it! Stop yelling at each other!"

Adam saw the turmoil in his son's face and felt tears sting at the back of his eyes. It was like looking at a reflection of himself twenty years ago. He looked down at his fisted hands leaning on the desk and then at Meagan who had stepped back, but was still stiff with anger. They were two combatants, just like his parents had been. This couldn't go on. He had to put a stop to it right now.

Taking several deep breaths, he forced himself to relax and sit back down. He was relieved to see that Meagan did the same thing. "I'm sorry, buddy. Miss Meagan and I got carried away. It won't happen again."

Meagan put her hand out to Jason and he walked over to her. She hugged him. "Your dad's right. Sometimes adults can act pretty dumb, but we're finished acting that way. Okay, tiger?"

Jason nodded. Meagan turned to Adam. "Are we finished? I'd like to get some writing done before bedtime."

Adam felt like lead resided where his heart had a moment ago. Shaking his head, he said, "No, I'm sorry, but there is just one more item we need to discuss."

Meagan's eyes narrowed, but her voice was calm. "Fine."

Adam smiled at his son. "Could Miss Meagan and I have a few more minutes of privacy?"

"You promise not to fight anymore?"

"We promise." Adam said the words knowing that soon Jason would be just as upset as he had been when he discovered them fighting. Neither Jason nor Mandy were going to take the news of Meagan's leaving well, but it had to be done. She brought too much upheaval to all their lives.

&

Meagan felt the last vestiges of her anger drain out of her as Adam promised not to fight with her anymore. Fat chance. Arguing was part of life. No one agreed about everything. It would probably be best to avoid shouting. However, one thing she had learned growing up in a house with Irish parents and more sisters and brothers than the average child, was love could get loud and so could anger. The important thing was to keep the scales heavily balanced on the side of love and joy.

Adam waited until Jason left the room and shut the door before speaking again. "Meagan, I'm not sure how to say this, but I don't have any choice."

Was he going to apologize after all? "Say what?"

"This is not working."

Pain welled up inside Meagan like a geyser, choking her. He sounded exactly like Brian when her ex-husband had told her their marriage was over. She heard herself repeating the same response to Adam almost word for word. "What isn't working?"

"You, me, this situation."

Oh, Father. She wanted to lean forward and grab her knees, keening in anguish. He was telling her she had to leave. How could this be happening again? She couldn't be losing Adam and his children, not over a simple misunderstanding.

Somehow she managed to remain upright in her chair. "Please be more specific. What exactly are you saying?"

"Meagan, I have to let you go. I can't have my family disrupted by chaos."

"One morning's mistake does not equal chaotic disruption, Adam."

He pushed the papers on his desk into a perfectly aligned pile, moving them until their edges were even with that of the desk. "It's not all your fault. Our views on life and child rearing are too different. I need a nanny that has views more in line with my own. My children deserve peace in their home."

That's all she was? Just a nanny? She loved Adam more than she had ever loved Brian and he saw her as just a nanny. She wanted to be the mother to his children and he thought of her as an employee to be disposed of when she inconveniently disagreed with him. Pain lanced through her like shards of glass cutting into her heart.

"What about Jason and Mandy? If I leave, they'll be devastated."

Adam turned to stare, transfixed out his window. "It's better now than later when they'll be even more attached to you."

"Just like private school?"

"Yes."

"I don't understand. Why? We were getting along great. I made a mistake not clearing the outing with you this morning, but I won't do it again." She stopped speaking as tears clogged her throat.

He turned back to face her and the pain she felt was mirrored in his eyes. "I'm trying to explain. Life with Caroline was difficult because we didn't have the same priorities. Jason and Mandy paid the price for that. I can't let that happen again."

Turning words that Adam had used earlier on him, she said, "I'm not Caroline."

He flinched. "No. You are not." He rubbed his eyes like he had earlier that day. "You aren't their mother and at least this time I can undo the damage."

The words buffeted her. *You aren't their mother.* Meagan remained silent, unable to speak.

Adam sighed and stood up. His face became void of emotion and he clasped his hands behind his back. "I'm sorry.

You're just not a good fit for my family. I'll be glad to pay for your move back to Scottsdale or give you a reference for another nanny position here."

He made it sound like it was all just a business arrangement, like her heart wasn't breaking into a million little pieces.

"How long?"

"As soon as you can make arrangements. I'll pay you severance wages of course, but I think it will be easier on Jason and Mandy if it's a clean break."

"I'll go pack. I'll be ready to leave before dinner."

His gaze locked with hers. "I didn't mean tonight, Meagan. I'm not tossing you out into the street."

She shrugged. "You said you wanted a clean break." She stood up and headed for the door. Pausing, with her hand on the knob, she turned to face him. "Do you want me to help you tell Jason and Mandy? I'll want to say good-bye regardless."

"I'll tell them while you're packing."

She nodded and turned to leave the room.

Three hours later, her things were packed. Grateful now that she hadn't gotten around to having her boxes shipped up from storage, she picked up a large suitcase and her laptop. Taking one last lingering look around her room, she tried desperately to quell the tears spilling over her eyelids. She had to calm down before she saw the children. She refused to add to their sorrow by exposing hers.

She had almost finished packing her car when Adam and the children came out the front door. At the look of woe on Jason and Mandy's faces, she almost burst out sobbing right there. She held herself in check. One positive result of the divorce was that she now had better control of her emotions.

She would have lost her job if she had walked around crying all day.

Walking up to the front porch, she put her arms out to Jason and Mandy. Both children flew into her embrace and hugged her so hard she had difficulty breathing. She didn't mind. Mandy's voice came out muffled against her T-shirt. "I don't want you to go. I thought you were going to be my mommy."

A knife twisted in Meagan's heart. She had no answer for her small charge, so she said nothing. Jason lifted his head and swiped at his eyes. "You're the best nanny we've ever had."

Meagan smiled at him, her own eyes misty. "Thanks. You're the best children I've ever looked after."

"Will we ever see you again?" Mandy's voice sounded so forlorn that Meagan could not deny her.

She gave Adam a defiant look over his children's heads. "Yes, sweetie, you can count on it."

Adam's mouth tightened, but he didn't gainsay her. "Do you have anything else you need brought down?" His voice was void of emotion.

"Yes, there are a couple more things."

He turned to go. "I'll get them."

Meagan felt the two warm bodies crushed against hers and knew she had to say something to make this easier for them.

"Jason and Mandy, do you remember how you prayed for God to send you a different nanny?"

She felt two small heads nodding against her.

"He sent me, but now it's time for me to go. It's hard to understand, but sometimes we have to face really tough things in life. I know it hurts. But you have to remember, no one knows what the future may bring."

"I want you." Mandy's words were echoed in Jason's eyes.

Meagan gently set Mandy and Jason from her.

"I'm going to tell you two a story. Will you listen?"

The soft assurance in her voice must have gotten through, because both of them nodded.

"I used to be married."

Jason's eyes grew wide. "Did your husband die like my mom?"

"No, tiger. He didn't. We got a divorce and I thought I would never have the chance to love and care for my own children. Then God brought you two into my life and I was blessed beyond words. You trusted God to bring you a new nanny, will you trust him to take care of you now?"

"I'll try." Jason's voice was filled with sadness, but he sounded sincere. "Me too," agreed Mandy.

"Good, because my life will always be sweeter for knowing you. I want to think of your life being sweeter for knowing me, not more sad."

Adam came with her remaining bags. She opened the passenger door for him to place them in the front seat. He dropped the bags in the car and closed the door. Moving in front of her, he lifted her chin to look into her eyes. She could feel the heat of his body and smell the scent that was uniquely him. It infuriated her that she still reacted to his touch. "Where will you go?"

"Does it matter?"

His jaw hardened. "Yes. Of course it matters. I'm not doing this to hurt you, Meagan."

Jerking her chin from his hand, she stepped back. "I'd hate to see what happened if you tried, then."

Chapter Ten

Meagan pulled out of Adam's driveway, keeping him and the children in sight through the rearview mirror. Desolation washed over her as she drove away from the small family she had begun to think of as her own. Determined not to give in to tears again, she focused on finding her way to the main road.

Lord, what now? The simple plea was all she could manage. She didn't want to go to Jake and Patty's. Not yet. Her heart wasn't up to explanations or even the comfort that Patty would try to extend. Suddenly, she remembered the promise she had made to Ruth that morning. It gave her direction. Pushing the pain of Adam's rejection into the background, she headed for Christian Supply.

Their selection of Bibles would have intimidated her if she didn't know exactly what she wanted. A few minutes of searching and about forty dollars later, she walked out of the bookstore with resolution in her step. Stopping in the car, she took a few moments to write an inscription on the inside of the Bible's cover.

Although the evening was warm, Meagan shivered as she got out of her car in front of Ruth's motel. Gratitude that the summer days were still long washed over her. She would hate to come here in the dark. A group of young men tossed insults back and forth in the parking lot, a couple of them slouching against a rusty Impala. A barely dressed woman lounged against the wall of the motel talking to a man who glanced furtively over his shoulder every couple of seconds.

Clutching the bag with the Bible in it to her chest, Meagan knocked on Ruth's door. She prayed the young woman was home. She didn't want to come back. Noises came through the open window. Someone swore after bumping into a piece of furniture. A man's voice. Meagan's courage almost failed her and she contemplated high-tailing it back to her car when the door in front of her swung open.

"What do you..." Ruth's voice trailed off as her eyes widened with recognition.

Meagan smiled tentatively. "Hi. I brought that book we were talking about this morning." She lifted the bag for Ruth to see, Christian Supply's logo emblazoned on the side.

The man Meagan had heard through the window came up behind Ruth. He leered at Meagan and then turned to Ruth. "You read?"

"Of course I read. What, do you think I'm a moron just because once in a while I hang out with losers like you?"

The man's eyes narrowed. Pulling a couple of bills from his wallet, he tossed them at Ruth. She grabbed the money before it could fall to the floor. "It's losers like me that keep you in business, Baby, and don't you forget it."

Meagan hastily stepped back as the angry man pushed past her.

"Do you wanna come in?"

Meagan nodded and stepped forward into the motel room. The door closed behind her and it took a minute for her eyes to adjust to the dim light. The shades were drawn and a single lamp was on by the bed. Everything about the room was worn. The bedspread was faded, the sparse furniture scratched and dented, and the carpet looked like it had been there since before the Flood.

Along the wall next to the bathroom was an efficiency kitchenette with a dilapidated mini fridge, a two burner stove and a sink with rust stains. Meagan watched as Ruth opened the mini fridge and pulled out a container of cottage cheese. She opened it and put her fingers right into the small white curds. Pulling out a tiny zip lock bag, she smiled at Meagan.

"My savings account. I eat at the shelter so I can save more money. Someday, I'm gettin' out of here." The desperate certainty in her voice tugged at Meagan's heart.

Ruth folded the money her "client" had tossed at her into a small square and slid it into the little plastic bag. She put the bag back in the cottage cheese, closed the container and returned it to the fridge. Turning on the water in the rusty sink, she washed the white film from her fingers.

She opened a cabinet under the sink and pulled out a can of disinfectant and a can of room freshener. "I gotta go through my routine."

"Sure. Of course. Routine." Now who sounded like a moron, Meagan wondered.

Ruth sprayed the bed sheets with disinfectant, the nightstand and the small table and chair under the window. She then sprayed the air liberally with the room freshener.

"Do you mind hanging out a little while so I can take a shower?"

Meagan sat down in the newly disinfected chair. "No problem. Take your time." She didn't have anywhere to go.

Thrusting aside the depressing thought, she pulled Ruth's new Bible out of the bag and thumbed through it until she found the passage on Rahab. She had barely begun to read when the other woman came out of the bathroom wearing a loose T-shirt and biking shorts. Her orange hair was still wet and flat against her head.

"That was fast."

Ruth shrugged. "Yeah, well, I don't always have a lotta time between appointments, ya know?"

Meagan didn't know, but could imagine. "I'm sorry I interrupted you earlier."

Ruth sat down on the end of the bed. "Don't let it worry you. His time was up anyway."

Meagan didn't know what to say to that, so she didn't say anything. Instead, she indicated the open Bible in front of her. "This is where you'll find the account of Rahab."

Ruth leaned forward to see. "The chick was really in the business?"

"Yes, it says so right here." Meagan read a short excerpt out loud.

"I don't believe it. Can I see that?"

"Sure." As Meagan handed the study Bible to Ruth, she pointed out the separation between the actual Scripture and the notes.

"So, like, if I have a question I can read this stuff down here at the bottom and it will explain it?"

"Well, it will explain something. The best advice I can give about reading the Bible is to ask God to help you understand it."

Ruth dropped the book back on the table like it burned her. "You mean I gotta pray?" Her voice rose in protest.

Lord, please help me not to mess this up. "You don't *have* to do anything. But if you *want,* you can just ask God to help you understand. He promised to give wisdom to people who ask."

Ruth looked skeptical. "I don't know if I can do that."

"Repeat after me."

The look Ruth gave her led Meagan to believe the other woman doubted her sanity, but she agreed. "Okay."

"Lord, please help me to understand your Word."

Sounding self-conscious, Ruth repeated Meagan's words.

"Well, was that too hard?"

"That's all there is to it? I don't have to say any mumbo jumbo about thous and thees?"

"Nope."

Relief washed over Meagan when Ruth picked up the Bible again. "Okay, I guess I can do it."

A knock sounded at the door. Meagan jumped up. "It sounds like your next appointment is here."

Ruth looked longingly at the Bible before putting it back in the plastic bag and then placing the bag inside the cabinet with the disinfectant. Another knock sounded at the door, louder this time and accompanied by an impatient bellow. "Hurry up, Baby, I ain't got all night."

"I guess you gotta go. I probably won't see you again, will I?"

The words were so much like Mandy's that Meagan's eyes burned. She gave the other woman an impulsive hug. "Don't count on it. I don't disappear that easily."

After standing stiff for a second, Ruth returned Meagan's hug, whispering a thank you in her ear. Pounding on the door made them both jump.

"All right already!" Ruth opened the door.

Meagan left, skirting the irate man who stood outside. As she headed back to her car, the flashing neon sign that said vacancy caught her eye. Goose bumps broke out on her flesh. *Oh, no, Lord. You don't mean it. I can't stay here.* Almost of their own volition, her feet carried her to the motel office. Meagan heard herself asking about a room. The oily man behind the desk gave her the option of two. More goose flesh broke out on her arms. One of the rooms, the one with an air conditioner and a telephone, was right next to Ruth.

"I'll take it."

She paid for a week in advance and took the key attached to a diamond-shaped plastic key ring with the room number printed in large letters. Walking back outside, she took in her surroundings. Seedy was the best description for her new home. The difference between this dilapidated motel and Adam's farm was like comparing the skin of a newborn baby to that of his great-great grandmother.

She stopped at her car to pull out an overnight bag and her laptop before letting herself into her room. As she surveyed furnishings almost identical to those in Ruth's room, Meagan wished she also had a spray can of disinfectant.

Throwing her stuff onto the bed, she picked up the phone and dialed Patty's number. The phone was answered on the first ring.

"Hello?"

"Hi, Patty. It's Meagan."

She heard a huge sigh. "Meagan. Thank God. We've been so worried about you. When Adam called and told us what happened, we kept expecting you to show up or call. So did he. He's been calling every fifteen minutes for the past two hours. He's really worried about you."

"He fired me. I am no longer his concern."

"Don't be ridiculous. He was worried you were going to try driving home tonight."

She almost said she didn't have a home, but refrained. "I didn't."

"Where are you?"

"I'm staying in a motel for right now. I promised to help with VBS, remember?"

Ignoring Meagan's reference to VBS, Patty latched on to her former statement. "Why are you in a motel? You could have stayed with us."

"I know. It's just that I think God has different plans." Meagan told Patty about her visit with Ruth and the vacancy.

"You're staying in a motel that caters to prostitutes? Do you think that's wise?"

"I don't know, but I do know it's God's will."

That silenced Patty's protests. They talked for a few more minutes, Patty apologizing profusely for not warning Meagan about Adam's refusal to let Jason accompany them to the homeless shelter the year before.

"Don't be silly, Patty. None of this is your fault. Adam just decided I wasn't a good fit. He's probably been thinking along those lines for a while and this was as good excuse as any."

"I can't believe that. You fit his family like you were created just for it."

Patty's words stung and Meagan didn't want to deal with any more pain that night. "Look, I've got to go."

"All right, but give me your address and number."

Meagan rattled off the information, repeating the number twice for verification.

"Call Adam, would you? He really has been worried sick."

Meagan's hand clenched around the receiver. "That's not my problem."

Patty sighed again. "I'm sure you feel that way now, honey, but I still wish you'd call him. I think he's already regretting his decision to let you go."

Meagan gave a short, bitter laugh. "Not likely. He was very clear in his regimented way. I'd be surprised if he doesn't have a list of reasons why it was a good decision."

"Oh, honey." Patty's voice was full of sympathy.

"Look, if you're so worried about Adam's peace of mind, *you* call him."

"I doubt I'll have to. He's probably the one who's been trying to ring through for the last ten minutes."

After hanging up the phone, Meagan flung back on the bed and stared at the ceiling. She slipped into an emotionally exhausted slumber.

∓

Meagan was dreaming. She was in Scottsdale, lying in a lounger by her parents' pool. The sun was baking her skin. She turned over, but the heat emanating from the bricks below was as hot as the sun on her back. One of her nephews was pounding on the bricks with his building blocks. She was trying to tell him to stop, but no sound would come out of her mouth. Suddenly her nephew was talking to her, but he had Adam's voice.

"Meagan! Open the door. I know you're in there."

She came to a drowsy wakefulness. The pounding in her dream was still going on, only it wasn't on hot Arizona bricks. Someone was about to shake her motel room door off its hinges.

"Mind your own business. I'm here to visit my friend."

"Aren't we all, buddy? Keep it down. She'll get to you when she gets to you."

Meagan came more fully awake. Adam? Adam was outside her door and it sounded like he was having an altercation with one of Ruth's appointments.

She jumped off her bed and realized that she was bathed in sweat. She'd forgotten to turn on the air conditioner and the room was like an oven. Grabbing a washcloth, she wet it and wiped her face and arms quickly before opening her door.

Adam's hand, fisted to knock again, stopped in mid-air.

Another man spoke from near Ruth's door. "Finally. I tell ya, don't keep this john waiting again. He's about as patient as a sixteen-year-old kid."

Adam glared at the other man before shouldering past Meagan into her room. "Meagan, that man thinks you're a woman of the street. And he thinks I'm one of your clients."

She couldn't help it. She laughed. He was so outraged. "Don't let it worry you. I doubt you'll ever see him again."

"Neither will you. Get your stuff, we're leaving."

She stared, dumbfounded, at him. "Excuse me, but did you, my *former* employer, just order me to move out of my motel room?"

He didn't even pause. "Yes."

Slamming her hands on her hips, she took an offensive posture. "I'm not going anywhere."

"Meagan, do you realize what the woman next door does for a living? She's a streetwalker. That man standing there was one of her clients."

"I am fairly certain she is not a streetwalker." He looked somewhat mollified until she spoke again. "I think all of her clientele comes to her."

"Meagan do you know what you're saying?" His outrage was starting to wear thin.

"Surprising as it may be for you to believe, Adam. I am in fact aware of what is coming out of my mouth."

He didn't appreciate her sarcasm. She knew that when his nostrils pinched in anger. "I could swear there was a drug deal going on in the parking lot, too. What do you have to say to that?"

"I'd have to say that I'm not surprised. You may not have noticed, but this is not exactly the West Hills here, Adam."

"I don't think there is anything even remotely funny about this situation. Your mockery is misplaced."

All she wanted to do was shout at him. Not a good thing. Giving herself a minute to calm down, she reached for the air conditioner and turned it on. The fan started with a loud whir and a small blast of blessedly cool air issued forth.

Taking a deep breath and expelling it, she sat down on the edge of the bed. "Why are you here?"

"More to the point, why are you?"

"Don't answer a question with another question. Didn't anyone ever tell you that it's annoying?"

He grunted. "Thanks for the advice. Now tell me why you're here."

"Because you threw me out."

"Don't be foolish. I didn't throw you out. You insisted on leaving today. I told you to stay until you had made arrangements to leave."

"Well, I've made my *arrangements*."

Sweeping the room with a disdainful glance, he said, "You prefer this over staying with Patty?"

Who did he think he was to question her living accommodations? She glared at him. "It's not a matter of preferring it over Patty's home. I have my own reasons for staying here."

He looked ready to explode, but his question came out in that irritating quiet drawl he used when he was angry. "What are they?"

"Didn't Patty tell you? You must have spoken to her to have known where to find me."

Suddenly he found something very interesting about the picture on the wall above her bed. "I, um, I didn't give her the chance."

Things were looking a little brighter if Adam had come tearing over to the motel the minute he learned where she was. Maybe Patty was right and he regretted firing her. "Let me get this straight. Patty calls you—"

He interrupted. "I called her."

"Okay, you called Patty. She told you where I was and you rushed over here to save me from myself."

He grimaced and tugged on the middle button of his polo. "Yes."

"Why?"

His look of discomfort fled to be replaced by anger. He glowered at her. "That's a foolish question. What did you expect me to do?"

"What did I expect? Definitely not that you would feel the need or the inclination to take a personal interest in where I live. I'm just your former nanny."

"What does that have to do with anything?"

"You can't tell me that you've taken this kind of interest in your other nannies after they left your employ." *Please say no,* she thought. Show me that you care about me personally, at least a little.

He tugged at the bottom button on his polo. "Well, no, but you're different, Meagan."

The small spark of hope that had ignited when he admitted to hanging up on Patty to come rescue her, fanned into a small blaze in her heart. "I'm different? In what way?"

He pivoted and started prowling around the room. "You're undisciplined and free-spirited. You're bound to get yourself into trouble. Since your family isn't around to look after you, I'll have to."

Her spirits plummeted and her anger rose at his insulting reasoning for expressing concern for her well-being. It wasn't personal. He just thought she needed a keeper and since her family wasn't around to do it, he would. "How very kind of you."

His head snapped around at the sarcasm dripping from her words.

"I am almost twenty-eight years old. I've been divorced, had a successful career and am embarking on a new one. I do not, I repeat, do not require a babysitter, caretaker or big brother. So, if you are finished insulting me, do you think it would be too much to ask you to leave? I'm tired."

"I don't want you staying here. Come home with me. Please. If you don't want to stay with Patty, you can stay with us until you know what you want to do."

She knew the please had cost him, but she wasn't going to be swayed. "I already know what I want. I want to stay here. It's safer."

He stared at her as if he couldn't believe he had heard her correctly. "How could you possibly be safer here?"

She shook her head. He'd never understand, but she'd tell him anyway. "I'm talking about my heart, Adam. I'm not worried about my person. Thanks anyway."

Then, pushing him out the door, she closed it and leaned against it. He knocked again and she could feel the vibration in her heart. "I'm not giving up. I'll call you tomorrow. Maybe you'll be more willing to listen to reason then."

"Not likely, Adam, not likely." She didn't say it loud enough for him to hear through the door because she wasn't saying it for his benefit. She was saying it for her own.

୧୬

Adam was still fuming Sunday morning on the way to church. He had called Meagan every day since she left and she remained stubborn about staying in that rat-hole she called a motel. She wasn't even willing to explain why she chose to stay there. If he hadn't talked to Patty, he would have been convinced it was simply to thwart him. Patty had told him about some woman named Ruth that Meagan had taken a Bible to. Why Meagan had to stay in the motel to minister to Ruth was beyond him.

He found no comfort in the fact that her willingness to put herself at risk for her ministry to Ruth reinforced his belief that she might make similar choices for Jason and Mandy, putting them at risk in order to minister to others. Just like she had done by taking them to the homeless shelter. He didn't want to be right. He missed her and so did the children.

Last night, Mandy had woken from a nightmare, crying out Meagan's name. It had taken him nearly an hour to calm his daughter. The subsequent lack of sleep for them both was the reason that they were attending the late service, not because Meagan preferred it and would probably be there.

He ignored the rush of pleasure that he felt at the sight of her sitting and talking with another woman in the pew they routinely occupied. He reminded himself that she would have been with them the past few days if she hadn't been so stubborn about returning to the farm. *Or if you hadn't fired her.*

Jason and Mandy rushed forward to greet her like she had been gone a month, not mere days. She pulled them both into a bear hug. He could hear their excited chatter as he approached.

"Miss Meagan, you're here. I miss you so much. I had a bad dream last night and I wanted you."

Meagan's eyes met his and he read the accusation in them. His insides twisted in frustration and what might have been remorse. He wasn't sure anymore that letting Meagan go had been the right decision, or maybe the wrong decision had been the one to hire her in the first place. If he hadn't, neither he or his children, or Meagan for that matter, would be going through the pain of separation.

He sat down next to Jason, relaxing slightly as the worship music started. At least nothing else could be said. He could also avoid Meagan by focusing on the words to the music. He wished he could avoid his own thoughts. Images from the weeks with Meagan cascaded through his mind. He saw her tenderly touching Mandy. He imagined her head thrown back in laughter, the sun shooting sparks off of her fiery hair. When he remembered how she had taught Jason and Mandy biology by planting a flower garden, he knew he was lost.

I give up, Lord. I'll ask her to come back as our nanny. Adam expected peace to flow over him now that he'd made the decision, but it didn't. It still felt like he was missing something, only he couldn't figure out what. He refused to dwell on it. He would ask Meagan to come back and she'd stop living in that rundown excuse for a room.

After worship, Jake dismissed the children to their classrooms and Adam moved nearer to Meagan. She gave him a cool stare which he returned with a smile. "Don't rush away after service, there's something I need to ask you."

"I'm not going to listen to another lecture on my accommodations."

"No lecture." When she still didn't look convinced he said, "I promise."

She nodded once and then turned her focus on Jake and his sermon. Adam had a hard time keeping his mind on Jake when all he could think of was having Meagan safely under his roof again.

After service Patty invited them all to her house for brunch. "Now that I have a new kitchen, I might as well use it."

Adam turned to Meagan. "What do you want to do?"

"I'm going over to Patty's to finish the stuff for VBS with her later anyway, but somehow I think it would be less stressful for her if we didn't descend on her home. She's got so much to do for VBS I can't imagine she has the energy to cook for all of us." Funny how it seemed so natural for he and Meagan to discuss things like this. She definitely belonged back at the farm. She was an excellent nanny.

Patty tried to shush Meagan. "Nonsense. What are a couple more people for lunch?"

"Four is not a couple," insisted Meagan.

Patty looked like she was preparing to do battle when Adam forestalled her. "May I offer a compromise?"

Both Patty and Meagan gave him their full attention. "What if I picked up a bucket of chicken and the fixings? We'd still be enjoying your hospitality, Patty, but we wouldn't be running you ragged when you need all the energy you can muster for VBS."

Patty sighed in defeat. "I guess, but don't think I'll give in so easily next time."

"I wouldn't dream of it."

Jason and Mandy asked to ride with Meagan, and Jake offered to go with Adam to get the chicken. Patty went off to round up her teen offspring. If Adam hadn't made the decision to rehire Meagan he would be dreading the ride, but now he actually looked forward to talking things over with his friend and pastor.

After Jake had folded his tall frame into the Volvo's passenger seat, Adam opened the conversation. "Before you read me a lecture, let me tell you I already decided to ask Meagan to come back to the farm."

"A lecture, huh?"

"Don't think I missed that look Patty gave you before you offered to come with me to get the chicken."

Chuckling, Jake nodded. "You know my wife, all right."

"Actually, until I met Meagan, I had no idea what a meddler Patty could be."

"They've been friends a long time."

A comfortable silence fell until they had almost reached the restaurant. "So, do you mind my asking what changed your mind?"

"I was wrong. I told Meagan that she wasn't a good fit with our family, but the fact is she's perfect. I've just got to be more careful in the future to let her know what I want Jason and Mandy doing."

Jake rubbed his chin. "Hmm. I see. And if she doesn't agree?"

Adam darted a surprised glance at Jake. "She's my nanny. She may not agree, but she'll go along. After all, Jason and Mandy are my children." Remembering the way she threw herself into homeschool, he was surprised Jake would question her willingness to do what she needed to be a good nanny.

They arrived at the drive-through and Adam ordered their meal. The smell of chicken and gravy filled the car. Jake rubbed his stomach. "Smells mighty good. Preaching builds an appetite."

It was Adam's turn to laugh. "You don't fool me. When it comes to chicken, for you doing anything builds up an appetite."

"You've got my number, all right."

Adam pulled into the circular drive in front of Jake's home and parked his car. Jake hefted two of the plastic bags full of food from the backseat. "I'm glad you're going to ask Meagan to come back to the farm. I wouldn't want to have to face Patty otherwise. Now, she'll think I'm a pretty good advisor."

Adam smiled at Jake. "Me too. We all miss her and the thought of her living in that motel has kept me awake at nights." He retrieved the rest of the food before locking the car.

"I'll be praying for you."

"Thanks. I have a feeling I'll need it."

"So do I." Jake's tone was much more serious than Adam's had been.

Adam gave his friend a searching look, but Jake was already smiling in greeting at his wife.

An hour later, everyone had eaten their fill. Jason and Mandy played croquet on the lawn with Jake and Patty's teenage sons. The adults lounged around the patio table, chatting. Adam stood up and asked Meagan if he could speak to her in the house.

She gave him an uncertain look, but agreed. Winking at Patty, he led Meagan into the living room. Meagan took a seat in one of the matching wing chairs near the fireplace. Adam sat down in the other.

"Jason told me that you gave them the rest of the summer off from school."

"Yes. It was sort of a given, not having a teacher." Meagan said nothing. "Jason's going to plant a pumpkin patch and Mandy plans to spend her time learning to skate better than Lucy Miller."

That elicited a smile from her. It didn't last long. Her expression turned mutinous. "I'm really not going to listen to another lecture about where I live."

"I promised."

"Then what do you want to talk to me about?" She sounded impatient. He hoped Jake was praying.

"I won't prolong this, Meagan. I was wrong when I fired you and I want you to come back to the farm."

"You want to rehire me?" Far from sounding elated, like he expected, Meagan was wary.

"Yes."

"For how long?"

The question stymied him. "How long?"

"Yes."

His confusion cleared. "You want a written contract. Fine. What time frame do you want stipulated? I've always had month to month—"

Meagan cut in. "I'm not talking about a written contract."

"You're not?"

"No."

He was confused again. What was she asking?

"I want to know what happens the next time I make a mistake or do something you don't like."

"I think we can safely avoid another occurrence like the last one."

"How?"

"I've learned my lesson as I'm sure have you."

"What lesson is that?" Her tone was curious, but only mildly so. Something was wrong. This interview wasn't going the way he had expected. For one thing, she hadn't agreed to come back yet.

"I learned that I have to be more specific about my expectations."

"You mean it's possible to get more regimented than you already are?"

He let that slide. She was still a little angry. He didn't blame her. He fired her for a mistake. The time had come to make amends. "I'm sure you'll be more careful in the future to ask my permission before doing anything with the children."

"Hmm. That's an interesting thought. Am I supposed to ask permission before taking them to the mall, the park, the bathroom?"

He was starting to get annoyed. "Of course not. Only about important things like going to the homeless shelter."

"I can't read your mind, therefore I can't guarantee I would know what was important to you. In short, I think a repeat of what happened last week is inevitable. What I'm asking you, is what will happen when it does?"

He didn't have an answer for that. "I'm not convinced that it will."

"Well, I am and I'm not willing to risk the outcome."

Disbelief warred with an overwhelming sense of loss in him. "Are you saying you don't want the job?"

"I think you're finally getting the picture." She met his eyes, her hands gripped in tight fists. "Leaving this time hurt, but I survived. I'm not sure I would again."

Chapter Eleven

Another carrot went careening to the floor as Meagan's thoughts wandered back to the previous day's discussion with Adam. "Shoot." She stooped down, retrieved the carrot and rinsed it in the sink. There was no way she would have the snacks ready for over two hundred hungry munchkins on time if she kept losing track of her thoughts and the vegetables. Giving up on the carrots for now, she started making sandwiches. Bread didn't roll.

Saying no to Adam had been one of the hardest things she had ever done, but what choice did she have? After a week of learning to live without him and the children, she wasn't going to open herself up for more heartache by coming back. It would be different if Adam had even a smidgen of the feelings for her that she had for him. Then it wouldn't be just a business arrangement and she wouldn't be so scared of further rejection. Because her feelings precluded her ever being able to see anything with him as a simple business arrangement again.

Glancing at the clock, she wondered where her helpers were. Patty had told her that they were supposed to arrive over twenty minutes ago. Children were going to end up gnawing on whole carrots if someone didn't show up soon to help her slice them.

She was starting on a second plate of sandwiches, when Adam walked in. The plate of sandwiches tipped precariously, but she managed to hold on to them.

"What are you doing here?" came blurting out of her mouth before she could stop herself.

Raising his left eyebrow, he gave her a half smile. "Am I to take it that you not only object to being my nanny, but to my presence as well?"

Heat stole into her cheeks. "Of course not. You just surprised me. I've been tearing around trying to get stuff done without my helpers. I don't know where they are." Her voice babbled on, but she wasn't sure what she said.

Her attention was riveted on the man standing in front of her. Unfortunately for her peace of mind, he looked too good to ignore in a moss green polo and walking shorts.

"I'm your helper today. They're going to send a teenager to help if they can spare one, later."

She was going to strangle Patty. "At the committee meeting last week, the chair told me I had two mothers already slated to help. What happened to them?" She knew her voice sounded accusatory, antagonistic even, but she couldn't help it. VBS was supposed to be fun, not a week of torture. Working next to the man she loved, whose kiss drove her almost beyond reason, but whose sole interest in her was as his children's nanny, was not her idea of a good time.

His shoulders lifted in a negligent shrug. "There are more children than expected and they needed extra teachers. Your helpers had to transfer to helping other classes while the ones who had familiarity with the program became teachers."

Yeah, right and pigs fly. Patty was going to get an earful later. "That still doesn't explain what you're doing here."

"Patty drafted me."

She knew it. "Why didn't you help in the classroom? You're a professor. And speaking of classrooms, what about your summer classes?"

"They're over. I don't have another class until September."

"I'm sure you would be more comfortable teaching than cutting up veggies and serving snacks to a church full of hungry children."

"I think I can handle cutting a few vegetables."

"Without losing any on the floor either, right?"

"What?"

"Never mind." Her brain was on overload. She sounded like an idiot. Forcing herself to calm down, she headed around the kitchen island. "Wash your hands over there and then you can start cutting these carrots into sticks."

"Fine."

"Great. I'll finish the sandwiches then." She opened one of the large stainless steel refrigerators and pulled out two more ten pound bags of carrots and several bunches of celery. She plopped them all down in front of him. "The carrots need to be peeled and the celery washed. Then cut them into small sticks."

He stared at the vegetables. She wanted to smirk. "Do we really need to cut all the vegetables for the week this morning? Won't they be fresher if we do them daily?"

Poor man, he hadn't known what he was in for when he let Patty manipulate him. Oh, well, volunteer beware and all that. "Those are just for today. Any leftovers, of course, will be saved for tomorrow, but I doubt there will be that many."

The next hour neither one of them spoke. Meagan busily prepared tray after tray of bite-sized sandwiches. Adam peeled and cut the carrots into uniform-sized sticks. He then placed them in the plastic bags, making sure each bag had an equal number of carrots. A woman could go crazy living with a man like that. She should be grateful she didn't have to deal with him on a daily basis.

She wasn't. She'd give anything to spend the rest of her life helping him loosen up. As tears pricked at her eyes frustration with her unstable emotions gnawed at her. She filled up the large water coolers with ice and poured filtered water over it. By the time she was finished with the second cooler, tears were running down her cheeks.

This was ridiculous. What was she going to do? If he noticed her crying, he'd want an explanation. She had no intention of giving him one. Turning, she hurried past him, intent on finding a private place to collect herself. He looked at her, surprised. When his gaze fell on her face his expression turned to concern.

"You're crying." He sounded shocked. He should be. There was nothing in the least tragic about making mini sandwiches.

She couldn't seem to stop herself from lashing out at him in sarcasm. "Nothing gets by you, does it?"

"Are you all right? Tell me what's wrong."

She shook her head. She couldn't explain. Adam was the source of her pain, but he'd hardly appreciate hearing that. Besides, she had no intention of laying her heart bare for him to reject. She rushed from the kitchen.

After spending ten minutes scolding herself about her display of emotion in a blessedly empty women's bathroom, she bathed her now dry eyes in cool water.

Lord, please help me. As prayers went, it lacked finesse and proper thanksgiving, but she was desperate. She was making a fool of herself and she hated it.

She re-entered the kitchen to find Adam slicing away at the vegetables. He'd made significant progress. She breathed a sigh of relief. No matter what her personal feelings, hungry children would be clamoring for their snacks very soon.

"I'll take up enough food for this first group and serve them. If you could finish the vegetables and bring me replenishment according to the schedule tacked on the wall behind you, everything should work out just fine."

He searched her face. She hoped all of her unruly emotions were now under control and that he saw nothing. "No problem, but I'll carry those water coolers out for you first."

She nodded her agreement before getting out a tray of sandwiches. He picked up one of the coolers and took it outside.

"Put it on this end please," Meagan said as she placed her platter on a table covered with a brightly colored tablecloth.

Adam placed the water cooler with the spigot over the edge of the table so that it would be easy to fill the small cups. "This all right?"

"Yes. Fine." She returned quickly to the kitchen to retrieve the vegetables and napkins.

He followed her and brought up the second water cooler. "Where do you want this one?"

Meagan indicated another, smaller table closer to the play area. "Over there. That one is for refills."

"Need anything else?" His eyes bored into hers, asking about more than the food.

She returned his gaze, her own steady. Tightening her ponytail she said, "Nothing else, thanks."

"You look like a teenager with your hair like that, Meagan." He put his hand out and gently pulled her hair.

"Hey! Watch it, buster."

He smiled and saluted. "Yes, ma'am." Walking toward the doors that led to the kitchen he said, "I'll keep to the schedule, Captain."

She gave him a look of mock severity. "See that you do."

The children started arriving and for the next three hours she had no time to think. They came in class groups in six shifts. Their steady chatter kept her mind occupied.

"What's in the sammiches? My mom says I can't eat peanut butter or liverwurst."

"Then you'd better have a brown sandwich. They just have butter and jelly."

"Do I have to eat the carrots? They make me hurl."

She laughed. "No, why don't you take celery instead."

"Can I have three sandwiches and one carrot stick?"

Everything went well, but she was worried about Adam running himself ragged. He not only brought up the food, but also kept the water replenished and obviously finished cutting the vegetables, because they didn't run out. No teenager had shown up to help. The afternoon was a blur of activity and when Meagan returned to the kitchen, she felt the distinct need to sit down for a moment.

Looking around the kitchen, she thanked the Lord for Adam's thoughtfulness. There wasn't a vegetable peeling anywhere. She had very little left to do. She would rinse the water coolers and wash the sandwich trays and vegetable bowls before returning to her motel room. Adam must have gone. Relief and disappointment battled for supremacy in her emotions.

She relaxed in a chair, resting her feet on a small stepstool. Weariness poured over her. Between the lumps in her mattress and thoughts of Adam, she hadn't gotten much sleep in the

169

past week. She closed her eyes for a momentary respite and leaned her head back against the counter. It felt good.

"Hello, Sleeping Beauty, or should I say Cinderella?"

Adam's warm voice startled her from her drowsy state. Her eyes flew open. "I thought you were gone."

"There are still dishes to wash." He indicated the platters stacked near the sink.

"I'll take care of it. You need to pick up Jason and Mandy. VBS will be over for the day soon."

She stood up and stretched, reaching her fingers high above her head. She groaned as her tired muscles protested against her movement. Clasping her hands and swinging them low in front of her, she noticed Adam watching her. His eyes fixed on her lips and she remembered the wonder of his kiss.

"I don't mind helping with the dishes, Meagan." His words took a moment to register.

Dishes. Right. "It will only take a minute. Go on. You don't want the children's teachers wondering where you are."

"When I sign up to do a job, I do it."

Secretly pleased by his stubborn insistence on remaining with her and helping with the dishes, she agreed. "Then let's get to it." She went to the sink and started filling it with warm water. After adding dish soap, she started wiping the platters with the sudsy water.

As Adam rinsed and dried the dishes, he started singing a silly song from one of Mandy's videos. Meagan laughed. "You won't believe this, but Patty told me both her boys have all the songs from that video memorized."

"I believe it. They're catchy tunes."

Meagan rolled her eyes. "Right."

"Are you criticizing my choice of music?"

Giving him her best wide-eyed innocent stare, sudsy hands to her heart, she asked, "Who me?"

"Yes, you."

Batting her lashes she simpered. "Why no. Your choice of music is elevated just like your taste in everything else."

The laughter drained from his face to be replaced by something else, something much more unsettling. He wanted to kiss her. She could see it in the rich chocolate depths of his eyes and they were glued to her lips. He leaned forward. Her breath caught in her chest. Their lips barely met.

"Daddy, want to see what I made?" Mandy's voice broke the tension and the tentative kiss. Adam took a hasty step back.

As he pulled away, Meagan felt acute disappointment and dawning hope. Adam McCallister felt something for her, even if he didn't know it. He wanted her for his nanny, but she wanted something more, something permanent and she wasn't going to give up without a fight.

As the middle child in a family of five children, she had a lot of experience at fighting for what she wanted. Her mother called it perseverance, her older sister said she was just plain obstinate. It didn't matter what you called it, it spelled eventual defeat for the walls around Adam's heart.

When she was eight years old, she'd wanted a girl's bike. Her parents had made it clear, however, that she would have to make do with her older brother's hand-me-down. It was a typical boy's bike, black with a red pin stripe.

Meagan wanted a pink bike with streamers coming out of the side of the handlebars and a white basket attached to the front. Her parents weren't moved by her protestations that girls didn't ride black and red bikes. So, she found ways to earn money, like weeding in their neighbor's garden and raking for her brother when he mowed lawns.

At fifty cents here and a quarter there, she had no hope of earning the money for a brand new bike. She did, however, earn enough for a can of pink metal paint, glittery streamers and a white basket.

No, she wasn't the giving up kind. After the divorce she had almost given up her dream of being a mother. She had been willing to settle for being Jason and Mandy's nanny. She wasn't settling any longer. She might have to alter her hopes and dreams, but she wasn't giving them up altogether.

છ

It was too early to be going to the church. Every muscle in Adam's body protested against being up, but he wouldn't leave Meagan to prepare for today alone. She had to be every bit as tired as he was after three days preparing and serving snacks to hordes of hungry children. In all probability she was even more exhausted. She usually arrived at the church long before he did.

Estelle interrupted his thoughts. "I look forward to seeing Señorita Meagan again."

"I'm sure she will be ecstatic to see you, Estelle. She's running herself ragged preparing and serving food with only my help."

"This is not good."

"No, it is not."

Meagan had earned Estelle's staunch support immediately after his housekeeper returned from her daughter's. Estelle had been mortified that she had mistaken Meagan for the nanny from the agency. Meagan refused to let her worry about it, going so far as to request his housekeeper teach her some Spanish so it could not happen again. Everyone had laughed and Estelle's admiration had not wavered since. She hadn't spoken to Adam for two solid days after he fired Meagan.

He wanted to get to the church before Meagan, but when they arrived in the kitchen she was already there, cutting apples. She looked like she hadn't slept much the previous night. Purple smudges were not completely hidden by make-up under her eyes. Anger surged through him. She was so stubborn. How did she expect to get any sleep as long as she insisted on staying in that motel? He knew it wasn't doing anything for his ability to rest.

Tamping down his anger, he summoned a smile. "Hi, I thought I'd bring the crew to help today."

Estelle and the children wanted to jump right in. Meagan assigned Mandy the job of putting the ice in the water coolers. She told Jason to fill them from the jugs of water. She thanked Estelle profusely for coming before letting her take over the job of slicing apples.

Turning to him, she said, "Adam, you can slice the mini pocket bread in half. I'll make the sandwich fillings."

He couldn't resist teasing her. Her smile was addictive. "You expect me to work? Some kind of thanks I get for bringing you help."

"I'm a slave driver. Now get to work, Mr. McCallister, before I have to dock your pay."

"It doesn't take a math professor to figure out that half of nothing is still nothing."

"Your knowledge of numbers is so impressive." She spoke in a baby voice filled with humor. Clasping her hands in front of her, she gave him an obviously over-the-top melting gaze.

Her attempt at flirtation was an unqualified success, just like every other attempt over the past few days. He felt his

173

insides tighten and a strong desire to pull her into his arms for a long and satisfying kiss. This constant urge to touch or kiss her was getting to him. He hated to admit it, but her staying at the motel actually might be safer.

The rest of the day flew by. When VBS was over, he wasn't ready to let Meagan go back to her motel room. With a little persuasion, he was sure she would agree to accompany him and the children to the aquatic center. He waited until they were all together in the kitchen before suggesting it. As he expected, Jason and Mandy did all the persuading. Meagan was no match for their pleading.

"But my suit is in my room back at the motel."

"We'll pick it up on the way."

"What can I say? Between you and the children, you've decimated my every objection." She didn't sound disturbed by the fact. "Where are we going swimming?"

"I thought we'd go to the place with the water slides." Jason and Mandy let out whoops of approval. From the grin on Meagan's face, he'd have to assume she liked water slides as well.

It didn't take long to drop off Estelle and pick up his and the children's swimsuits and towels. Then they headed for Meagan's motel. She stopped to greet the man he'd seen making a drug deal on his first visit. He should be angry, but he wasn't. That was Meagan. If he asked, she'd probably tell him that she bought the drug dealer a Bible too. She came out of her room wearing a white T-shirt and denim shorts. It was a far cry from her usual neon colors and tie-dye.

Her smile added all the dazzle she needed to her outfit.

The pool was much more than just a waterslide. It was a new structure. The soaring ceilings and huge windows gave the impression of being outside. He insisted on paying for everyone, including Meagan.

"Better watch it, Adam, or I might get the wrong impression."

Turning at the sound of her voice, he asked, "What do you mean?" She had an impish grin gracing her features.

"If you're going to insist on paying my way, I might think this is a date or something." The idea was all too appealing.

Looking down at Jason and Mandy, he remembered the interrupted kiss in the church's kitchen. Smiling wryly, he said, "If it is, we have a couple of very effective chaperones."

She led Mandy to the women's locker room without answering. When they came out in their suits, he and Jason were already swimming in one of the five pools. Manufactured waves lapped around him as he watched Meagan and his daughter approach. She dropped her beach towel on a chair and he almost whistled. Her suit was emerald green and it clung to all the right places.

"Dad, I asked you a question."

Reluctantly, he shifted his gaze from Meagan to his son. Swallowing in his suddenly dry throat, he asked, "What was that?"

"I wanted to know if I could go down the water slide?"

"In a bit. Why don't you play on your tube for a while first?"

"Okay." Jason waved at Meagan and Mandy. "Come on. Dad rented some inner tubes. There's one for each of us."

Meagan smiled. "Thanks, Adam. I can't think of anything I'd rather do than just relax on an inner tube right now."

He could think of a few things, but he wasn't about to name them. He needed to rein in his wayward thoughts.

Tossing a tube to Mandy, he held Meagan's, waiting for her to come to him.

He pulled it toward her as she walked into the water, "I'll hold it while you get on."

She smiled her appreciation. "I take back everything I said about you."

There she went flirting again and tying his insides up in knots. It was time to show Meagan that he could hold his own. "Let me tow you out into the deep."

"Wow, what service." She relaxed against the black rubber sides of the tube.

Her eyes drifted shut.

This was almost too easy. "Remember the water fight, Meagan?"

"Yes. That was fun, wasn't it? I didn't know if you'd fire me or join in." She smiled. "Maybe we should have been wearing swimsuits then."

"You're wearing one now." He could tell the moment she realized his intent. Her eyes flew open and her body stiffened, but it was too late. Her high-pitched scream was swallowed in the pool.

She came up spluttering. "That was a dirty trick, Adam."

He grinned at her. "You ain't seen nothin' yet, sweetheart." Taking advantage of her surprise, he dunked her.

She came up moaning. "Oh, I think I have cramp." She gripped her side and grimaced.

He felt terrible. She'd had an exhausting week so far. He should have let her relax on her inner tube. "Are you okay? Where does it hurt?" He was bending over her in concern when she jumped up and pulled his head under water.

It was his turn to come up spluttering. Jason and Mandy screamed with laughter from their tubes nearby. "Think you're pretty smart, don't you?"

She nodded and then took off for all she was worth toward the other end of the pool. Jason and Mandy cheered her on. He chased after her. He could hear her screech from under water when his fingers closed around her ankles and started pulling. She went under. She tried to turn around and get him, but he released her ankle and swam away.

By the time she caught up with him, he had her inner tube. He offered it to her. "Friends again?"

She laughed. "For now."

Three hours later, they were all waterlogged. They had gone down the slides numerous times and Meagan had finally enjoyed several minutes of floating uninterrupted by his teasing or Mandy asking to go to the bathroom.

"What do you say, troops, who's hungry?"

"Me," Meagan and the children all chimed together.

Adam smiled at her. "So, trying to drown me gives you an appetite."

She laughed and nodded. "And then some."

"Sounds like a barbecue night to me."

Meagan groaned. "Adam." She drew out his name like it had five syllables. "I don't think I can wait that long."

He laughed at her. "I didn't mean that I planned to barbecue, sweetheart. There's a restaurant not too far from here that serves up Texas-style barbecue. The kids love it. I'm sure you will too."

"That sounds great." Her voice was breathless. He wondered why.

"Right. Let's get dressed. Don't keep us boys waiting. We know how you girls can be in the locker room."

"Right, Daddy. Jason always takes longer than me in swim lessons."

Meagan smiled. "We'll make it a race. Losers eat crow."

They all dashed for the locker rooms.

"Whew, we did it," Mandy exclaimed when she and Meagan arrived in the lobby.

He and Jason stepped out from their concealment around the corner. "Not likely, squirt. We've been out here for at least five minutes."

"Daddy, you scared me." Mandy sounded accusing, but giggled when Adam picked her up and pretended to feed her crow.

"Daddy, you still smell like the swimming pool." Mandy's words triggered a look of scrutiny from Meagan.

"You two didn't shower, did you?" She shook her finger at Adam. "For shame, Adam, one should never give up one's cleanliness even for the sake of winning should one?" She sounded just like an old-fashioned school marm. Her impish smile and the mass of wild red curls springing around her face ruined the effect.

"She sounds just like Mrs. Peer." Jason's avowal made Meagan raise her brows.

"And you told me she wasn't a martinet, Adam."

He grinned and shrugged. "What can I say? She used proper English."

Meagan laughed. "Okay. Enough of this banter. My stomach is making embarrassing noises. I think it's time you fed me. If you don't, I just might get hostile."

"I'm shakin' in my boots. Can't you tell?"

"Is that the proper accent for this here restaurant yer takin' me to?" She did a fair imitation of a cowboy drawl.

"Sure 'nough." He turned and started walking with the rolling gate of a cowboy. He couldn't believe he was acting so uninhibited, but she had that affect on him.

Laughing, his children fell in place behind him and followed suit. He turned his head back toward Meagan. "You comin'?"

"Sure 'nough."

Adam was relieved that the restaurant wasn't as crowded as usual. Meagan had made it very clear she was really hungry. After eating, Meagan was so tired she was almost falling asleep at the table. After yawning loudly for the second time, he offered to take her home.

"Thanks. I think I'll sleep like a log tonight." He hoped so. He was tired of the violet bruises under her eyes.

He pulled up in front of her motel. Jason and Mandy had both succumbed to the motion of the car and were asleep in the back seat. He looked at them and was reminded of the night they had come back from Salem, the night he had kissed her. He turned to look at her and wondered if she was remembering it too. She confirmed it when she said, "Looks like you'll be carrying them both in tonight."

He nodded. "Yeah, I guess so." Then, because he couldn't help it, he asked, "Meagan, are you sure you won't come home with us?" He expected her to say no, but had to try anyway.

She gently touched his cheek. He wanted to put his hand over hers and hold it against him, savoring the feel of her fingers against his jaw. "I'm sure."

He sighed. "It was worth a try."

"It will be fine, Adam, don't worry. Besides, I'm too tired to pack up and move to a new motel."

"You're a stubborn woman."

"My mother says I know how to persevere." She spoke quietly.

"That's one way of putting it." He felt like laughing. He'd like to meet her mother.

"Good night, Adam." She turned and opened the door.

"Wait." She stopped and looked at him. "Give me your key. I'll go in and check your room for you while you wait with the children in the car." She looked like she was going to argue, but she didn't. Handing him the key, she relaxed back against her seat.

He opened her door and turned on a light. *Oh, Father God, thank you for leading me to keep Meagan with us this evening.* The room looked like a cyclone had come through. Her clothes were strewn all over and every drawer was open. Even the mini refrigerator had been ransacked.

The last thing he wanted to do was have her come and see the destruction. He wanted to protect her from it, but knew that he couldn't. He walked over to the car and motioned for Meagan to get out.

"Adam, what's wrong?" He didn't answer right away, but stood, staring at her. He wasn't sure what to say. How did you tell a trusting soul like Meagan that someone had broken into her room?

"Adam." She prompted him.

"Meagan, it looks like someone picked your lock and broke into your room." He felt pain just saying the words aloud.

"Someone broke into my room?" Disbelief filled her voice. "You're kidding. They picked the lock? How could you tell?"

He put his hand on her arm and drew her close to him. "Your door was locked when I put the key in the lock. Your clothes have been tossed all over your room. It looks like they were searching for something."

She stared at him. "Adam, I..." Her voice trailed off without finishing whatever it was she had planned to say.

"Meagan, you're not staying here tonight. I checked your room and it's empty. Go in and pack your stuff." He hated the idea of her going into her room alone, but he couldn't leave the children in the car without supervision. "I'll take you back to the house. If you want to get a different motel room tomorrow, fine."

"Okay. You don't think we should leave everything and call the police?"

"We can if you want to, but I doubt they'll be able to do anything. Whoever was here is long gone. Someone broke into my friend's house last year and they still haven't recovered any of his lost property. I doubt they ever will."

She nodded, her expression dazed. She was gone less than ten minutes. "I didn't have that much in my room, just a few clothes. My laptop is in my car." Her voice was empty of emotion. She sounded like she was in shock.

He pulled her into his arms for a fierce hug. He almost missed the approach of a young man with stringy blond hair. He pulled away from Meagan and went to push her slightly behind him. Not unexpectedly, she resisted.

"Meagan, I'm sorry, man. I'm sorry."

Meagan pushed around Adam to stare at the man speaking. "You did this, Rick? I don't understand. Why? Why destroy my make-up? Why throw my clothes around?"

"They were looking for drugs. You can hide 'em almost anywhere." He gave a hollow laugh.

181

"They thought this was your room, didn't they? Oh, Rick, what if they had found you? Would they have hurt you?"

The young man shrugged. "I don't know. People will do anything for drugs, man. They'll even sell 'em to their friends to make money to buy their own."

He sounded lost. Surprising compassion for the younger man filled Adam. Meagan stepped forward. She said, "Listen, Rick, go home to your parents. Let them help you. You told me your mom is a Christian. She's praying for you. I know it. Please, go to her and let her help you. Does she live in town? I'll drive you there."

Adam wanted to laugh, but was afraid it would come out more of a sob. Her room had just been ransacked and she wanted to take care of Rick. If she thought he was going to let her drive Rick anywhere, she was fantasizing.

Rick was staring at her like she was a saint, not an overly trusting, too tenderhearted woman. "You wanna help me? After someone trashed your room because of me? Man, you're wild."

"Please, Rick. You have to get out of this lifestyle before you end up smashed like my favorite eye shadow."

"My mom lives in California. But thanks anyway."

Adam knew what was coming, so he forestalled it. "I'll buy you a bus ticket home if you leave tonight. Get your stuff together and I'll take you down to the terminal."

Now Meagan was looking at him like he was the saint.

Rick's eyes widened and he gave Adam a huge grin. "Sure, man. I'll be ready in a jif."

"Okay. But, Rick?"

"Yeah, man?"

"Flush your drugs down the toilet. Don't take them with you. Make a clean start right now."

Rick stared at Adam. "Man, I'll try, but pray for me."

"You can count on it."

Adam nodded his agreement. Rick smiled and looked like the carefree teenager that he should be. He turned and went to his room.

Adam turned to her. "You're a piece of work, you know that?"

"Thanks. You are too. I appreciate what you're doing for him."

"If I didn't, you'd probably offer to drive him to California on your way to Arizona."

Her smile died. What had he said?

"Believe it or not, I'm not that naïve." She didn't sound offended, just sad. What was going on?

"Glad to hear it. Will you drive the kids home in my car? I'll use your car to take Rick to the bus station."

"Sure, that's great. I really appreciate you doing this."

"You said that already. I'm not just doing this for you. I'm doing it for him too. Who knows, it might actually make a difference." He knew he sounded cynical, but he'd seen too many failed attempts by his father to change to believe that anything short of a miracle was going to change Rick's life. Maybe that miracle was waiting for him in California. Adam hoped so.

He took Meagan's suitcase and loaded it in his trunk along with her empty make-up case. "You going to be all right?"

"Yes. I'll see you at home."

Home sounded so sweet on her lips. He nodded. She got into the driver's seat and started the engine. "Be careful. Downtown is not the safest place for a college professor dropping off an ex-drug dealer."

He smiled at her turning the tables on him. "If you're worried about me, pray for me."

"Always, Adam, always."

She handed him the key to her room. "I almost forgot. Would you mind turning this in for me? I paid in advance and I don't really care about getting a refund. I just don't want to deal with anything else tonight." She sounded embarrassed by the admission.

He took the key. "Sure. I have a few things I'd like to say to the manager about security anyway."

"Don't be too hard on him. You haven't said, 'I told you so'. Thank you."

He touched her cheek. "This isn't about being right or wrong, Meagan. I'm just glad you were with me when they broke into your room."

His voice vibrated with emotion, but he couldn't help it. The thought of what could have happened if she had been there sent cold chills up his spine.

Chapter Twelve

Meagan could not seem to relax. Even the familiarity of her room in Adam's house could not dispel the horror she had felt upon walking into her motel room and finding it violated. Her ear was attuned for the sound of Adam's return. She loved what he was doing for Rick, but she needed the security of his presence.

The small lamp on the bedside table bathed the room in a warm glow. The break-in seemed unreal here. She sighed as she unpacked the clothes that she had hastily shoved into her suitcase. She piled them on the bed, intending to wash them. Perhaps if she could clean her clothes of the touch of the vandals, some of the dismay she was experiencing would dissipate.

Fighting an unreasonable fear of going downstairs alone, she took her clothes to the utility room near the kitchen. The slightest noise startled her. The old house was full of them as it settled for the night. She turned on lights as she went. By the time she reached her destination, almost every light in the house was on.

She opened the washing machine and was relieved to find it empty. Paying no attention to separating out her colors or delicates, she threw everything in at once. The rush of water filling the tub was a reassuring sound. It was so normal.

She went back upstairs to her room, leaving the lights on downstairs. She hoped Adam didn't mind, but she couldn't bring herself to turn them off. She sat on her bed. She barely got out a prayer of thanksgiving for her safety around the tight ball of emotions in her chest. Tears came and she couldn't stem their flow.

"Meagan? Are you all right?" Adam's voice, filled with concern, punctured the fog surrounding her brain. "I knew I shouldn't have left you alone."

She looked up at him, shaking her head. He had done what he had to for Rick. She wanted to reassure him, but couldn't get the words out.

He walked into her room and pulled her into his arms. "It's all right, sweetheart, go ahead and cry it out."

She couldn't help clinging to him, although her weakness embarrassed her. She sagged against him, soaking in his strength. "Adam, wh-what if I had been there?" Once the words were out she realized that's what had been bothering her. She had stubbornly insisted on staying there against Adam's advice. If he hadn't come with the children to take her swimming, who knew what would have happened to her?

"Sweetheart, God protected you. He planted you there for Ruth and Rick, but when you were in danger—He protected you." His words were like a balm, soothing her and bringing her peace.

"He did protect me. Oh, Adam, I don't deserve His mercy, but it's mine just the same."

His soft laughter surprised her. She looked up at him accusingly. What did he think he was doing laughing at her when she was crying? She glared at him. "I don't see what's so amusing about this situation."

"Meagan, it's just that none of us deserves His mercy. It's like Faith 101. A no brainer."

He could at least have the decency not to point out the obvious. "You're implying that I'm a simpleton and I'm supposed to be comforted?"

"No, you're supposed to feel comforted because I have my arms around you. What I say isn't supposed to matter."

She didn't appreciate his humor, but it was the truth. Just having him hold her was solace to her tattered nerves. She desperately wanted to snuggle closer and forget everything but how wonderful it felt in his arms. Her own frantic need for his touch scared her. It would be a poor idea to get too comfortable. He thought she was moving back to Scottsdale, and it didn't sound like he minded the prospect at all.

She stiffened in his arms and pushed herself away from him. He looked down at her but did not release her. His eyes were filled with laughter and another emotion she couldn't name.

"What's the matter?"

She wasn't about to tell him the truth and she didn't want to lie, so she ignored his question. "It's time for bed. We both need our rest for VBS tomorrow."

"Don't you want to know about Rick?"

In the stress of her roiling emotions, she had almost forgotten. "Definitely, but make it quick. We both have to be up early to prepare snacks for the hungry hordes tomorrow."

He smiled triumphantly and moved to sit down on the edge of her bed, pulling her next to him. "God was definitely in it, because the last southbound bus had been delayed due to engine trouble. I was able to get him a ticket and get him on the bus a few minutes before it pulled out."

Adam's faith wore feet. He didn't talk about doing the right thing. He did it. "That's great. I just pray that he can kick the drug habit."

He smiled at that. "Well, I gave him a jump start. I searched his bags and found a few items I didn't think he'd be needing when he got to his mother's."

"Was he angry?" She hated the idea of Adam putting himself at risk.

"No. He was actually pretty sheepish."

She sighed with relief. "Great. Did you turn in my key?"

"Yes, and I'll tell you all about my visit with your other neighbor if you come downstairs and have some tea with me."

She looked longingly at her bed, wanting the safety burrowing under the covers symbolized. Concern for Ruth won out. "Okay, but make it herbal. I don't want to be up all night." She was certain that she would have enough trouble sleeping as it was.

He smiled that killer smile he had and led her down to the kitchen. There was something different about him, but she couldn't figure out what it was. He seemed more relaxed, but that didn't make any sense after the evening they had been through.

She took a moment to put her wet clothes into the dryer before joining Adam in the kitchen. He had poured two mugs of steaming water from the hot water dispenser on the sink.

"Chamomile or Sleepytime?" He held up two boxes of tea bags for her to select from.

"Sleepytime." Maybe the herbal tea would help her mind to stop racing.

He placed the mugs on the kitchen table and sat down. She looked at him warily. She didn't know how to take him in this mood. She slid into the chair across from him and started playing with her tea bag, dipping it in and out of the hot water. She was overwrought. That was the only thing that explained the words that came popping out of her mouth. "Okay, did she proposition you, or what?"

His eyes widened in surprise, but didn't lose their amused gleam. "You sound surly. Would you mind if your neighbor propositioned me?"

She wasn't falling into that trap. "Of course I'd mind." His gratified look turned to one of chagrin when she continued. "I'm hoping that she'll find the strength to leave her line of work and find another way to live."

He leaned back in his chair, causing the two front legs to come off the floor and took a sip of tea. "Then I guess you'll like the message she told me to give to you."

"What was it?" The man could draw out his answer to the census taker on how many occupants lived in his house.

"She said to tell you that she thinks about that Rahab chick all the time. If God could change girlfriend's life, then he could change hers too. She was ready to show some real courage."

She could hear Ruth's voice through Adam's words and gratitude to God washed over her. "We discussed that real courage requires life changes."

His smile warmed her more than the hot tea. "That's great, Meagan. It's obvious that God had a plan for you going to the shelter when you did and staying in that motel."

Meagan felt a warm glow of peace steal over her. He wasn't castigating her for her foolishness. On the contrary, Adam seemed to have accepted that God had been working all the time, even when she took Jason and Mandy to the shelter. Suddenly, she was overwhelmed with fatigue. She knew she could sleep now and she wasn't afraid of nightmares. She yawned loudly. "I think it's time I hit the hay. How about you?"

"Sounds good. Morning is going to come awfully early tomorrow."

She nodded in agreement. As they made their way upstairs, Adam turned off the many lights she had turned on earlier. He didn't comment on it and she was relieved. She didn't want to try to explain her sudden fear of the dark.

As they reached the top of the stairs, she turned to him. "Thanks, Adam, for everything." He had taken care of her like she was someone precious to him.

"Any time, Meagan." He looked and he sounded like he meant it. She only wished he did. She chastised herself. *What happened to your resolve to fight?* She had to admit it had flown out the window when Adam made that comment about her driving Rick to California. He was obviously expecting her to return to Scottsdale soon.

And if he was expecting her to leave, then he couldn't want her to stay. It only made sense. Or did it? Honestly, in her exhausted state, she hadn't a clue.

℣

Meagan sat in the porch swing, pushing it back and forth slowly with her foot. She looked so relaxed, he hated to bother her, but he had promised the children. They had just gotten back from VBS and she hadn't even made a token protest about getting a room for the night. No doubt, she was too tired. She had really pushed herself this week and last night had to have drained her final reserves of energy.

"Hello, Adam. You've got that look."

He widened his eyes in an attempt at innocence. "What look would that be?"

"That look that says you're going to try to talk me into something. What is it?" She sounded wary.

"Jason and Mandy want to go to the park. I told them I'd ask you."

She groaned. "Where do they get the energy? I'm so tired, I can barely sit here."

She looked it. "I'll tell them you're too worn out." He turned to leave. She put her hand out to stop him.

"No. Tell them I'll be ready to go when I'm finished with this ice tea."

A rush of pleasure washed over him. He hadn't wanted to take the children to the park alone.

"Don't look so smug or I'll make you go too."

He stopped mid stride on his way in the house to tell Jason and Mandy. "What makes you think I'm not going?"

When they arrived at the park, the children scrambled out of the back seat almost before the car had stopped. Heading for a bench in the shade, Meagan turned her head to Adam. "Adam, I want to talk to you about something."

This sounded serious. Good. He had a few things he wanted to discuss with her as well. Yesterday's break-in to her motel room had been a wake-up call and he was tired of ignoring the alarm clock.

"Talk, I'm listening." She glared at him. He felt like smiling, but didn't. She'd been glaring at him a lot lately and he wasn't always sure he understood why. He'd better get used to it. Meagan was never going to be a dull companion.

"I don't think this idea of you taking a tenured position and moving to another state is a good one."

"I agree."

She acted like she hadn't heard him and plowed on. She must have been thinking about this a while. "I know how important security is to you, but at some point you have to just sit back and trust God. Are you sure this is part of His plan for your life?"

"No. I'm not." As a matter of fact he was so sure that it wasn't God's will that he had called the other college and turned down the job offer. His words must have finally registered because she stopped talking and stared at him in shocked silence.

"You're not? You do? Oh, Adam, I'm so glad. This has really been preying on my mind." She looked like she was ready to cry again and he thought she'd cried enough last night for his peace of mind. He didn't think he could stand it again.

"If you cry, I won't tell you what I do plan to do." As he expected, her tears dried up and her eyes filled with fire instead. "That's better. Your tears turn me inside out."

She stared at him like he wasn't making any sense. He was used to that. At any one time in his classes there were always at least a couple of students that didn't get it. That didn't stop him from lecturing and it wasn't going to stop him from talking to Meagan now.

"I called the dean of my department and told him about the offer and that I wasn't taking it. It shook him up that I had gone for the interview at all. He's preparing a proposal requesting tenure for me."

Her smile was radiant. "That's wonderful."

"Dad. Look at me." His son was standing on the top of the monkey bars. He felt his throat constrict.

"Jason, you get down from there right now." Meagan's bellow was loud enough that it started a child crying near them.
192

Adam wasn't surprised that she was just as concerned for his children as he was. That was one of the things they needed to talk about.

Jason shrugged and turned to climb down. His hand slipped and Adam watched helpless, as his son fell several feet to the ground. He felt as if it happened in slow motion. He could hear someone yelling Jason's name and only later realized that it was himself. He ran to the play structure and vaulted through the bars.

"Is he all right?" Meagan's voice sounded far away, but in reality she was right next to him.

Mandy was crying and in Meagan's arms. Other parents and children were asking if Jason was okay. If there was anything that they could do. He ignored everyone but his son, who lay still and lifeless on the ground.

He put his hand to Jason's chest. Thank God. He was breathing and his heart was beating a steady rhythm. None of his limbs were twisted at odd angles. He sent up a silent prayer of thanks for that as well. At least he had thought it was silent, but when Meagan joined her prayer to his he realized he must have spoken aloud.

"Yes, Father, thank you for your tender mercy. We pray that in every way right now you would protect Jason, lovingly caring for him as only our Divine Physician can."

Jason's eyes fluttered open. He looked confused. "Hi, Dad. I fell."

"I know, buddy." The sound of an ambulance could be heard in the distance.

His son's eyes widened. "Is that for me?"

"Yes, one of the parents called 911 when you fell. Don't worry. They'll just want to check you out. It's nothing to be afraid of." He knew that he said the words for his son as much as he said them for himself.

The ambulance pulled into the parking lot. The EMTs came quickly with their medical equipment. One of them gently asked Adam to step back while they checked Jason for spinal injury. His son looked so small and fragile as one of the paramedics placed a brace around his neck and told him to lie as still as possible.

"We'll want to take him to emergency to check more thoroughly for spinal injury. Nothing appears to be broken, though."

The paramedic smiled at him and Adam felt himself start to breathe more normally. "That's fine. Do what you need to do. Would it be better if I rode in the ambulance with him?"

"Sure. That will help him not be so frightened."

They brought the stretcher over and placed Jason on it. They wheeled it back to the ambulance. As Adam moved to follow the stretcher inside, Jason spoke. "Dad, would it be okay if Mom rode with me?"

Adam stared at his son. He wanted Caroline? Had the fall caused him to forget that she was dead? He hated having to remind his son of the loss, but there was no way he could fulfill his request.

"I'm sorry, buddy, it'll have to be me this time."

"But, I want Mom. Please." His son's lip started to quiver and Adam knew Jason was distressed. Jason hated to cry, especially in front of strangers.

The paramedic motioned for Adam to step out of the ambulance. "Maybe you should get his mom."

Adam tried to keep his voice low so that Jason wouldn't overhear. "I can't. My wife has been dead for two years. He must be confused by the fall."

Meagan walked up, holding Mandy's hand. "I'll drive Mandy over to the hospital and meet you there."

Adam was about to agree when Jason called from his stretcher. "Mom, I want you to ride with me. Let Dad take Mandy to the hospital. Please, Mom."

Meagan stared at Adam, concern filling her eyes. Jason was calling her mom. Thank God. This he could do.

"Just play along for now. Do you mind? I think the fall confused him."

She shook her head, not speaking at first. She cleared her throat as if it was obstructed by something. It was then he noticed the tears she was trying to blink back. "No, of course not. I'll see you at the hospital."

Meagan climbed into the ambulance and the paramedic followed her, closing the door on his son lying on a stretcher with Meagan holding his hand. The ambulance exited the parking lot, blue and red lights flashing.

∞

The doctor insisted on keeping Jason overnight for observation when he discovered that the boy was calling his previous nanny "Mom". Meagan spent the next two days trying to stay sane while supporting Adam and dealing with a surprisingly tearful Mandy. She understood Mandy's concern for her brother's fall and trip to the hospital, but even after Adam assured his daughter that Jason would be fine the little girl continued to cry at the drop of a hat. She made several comments about things going wrong. When Meagan tried to get her to explain, she closed up tighter than a clam.

Meagan was at her wit's end by the time the doctor decided it would be safe to send Jason home. Thankfully, once Mandy saw her brother in his own bed resting, she calmed down. She was in there with him now, reading old Archie Comic Book Digests. Meagan had gone in search of peace and quiet. She found it, curled up on the sofa with her Bible and journal in the living room. She took a sip of water before putting her glass down on a coaster on the end table.

Picking up her pen, she chewed on the tip, while she contemplated what to write in her journal. What words could best describe the last harried days, her emotional turmoil and the fear she had that Adam was going to send her merrily on her way once everything settled down? He hadn't said anything, but she hadn't forgotten his comment to Rick and he had certainly not alluded to the future in any way.

"Writing your impressions of the last few days for posterity?"

It was as if her thoughts had conjured up his voice. It took her a moment to realize that Adam was really there, smiling down at her in that "I've got you cornered now" manner. The last time he'd looked that way, he had convinced her to go to the park with him and the children. And look how that had turned out.

"Whatever it is, you can forget it. I'm not buying. I am going to sit on this couch and write in my journal and relax until dinner."

His laughter rippled over her, deep and masculine. Darn. She wasn't going to give in, no matter how irresistible he was. "I mean it."

"All I wanted was to talk to you. We've been too busy to say more than hi and goodbye the last two days."

"Imagine that. Your son has been in the hospital. He's still calling me Mom—"

Adam interrupted her tirade. "That's one of the things I wanted to talk to you about."

She nodded in understanding. "Don't worry. I already talked to the doctor. He told me it was better to humor him in hopes that he'll snap out of it on his own."

Adam's eyes darkened in concern. "I hope he's right. When I told him how attached the children are to you and that you had recently left, the doctor thought that explained Jason's confusion. He said it had been stress induced."

She couldn't stop herself from putting her hand out to comfort him. "I'm sure he's right. Jason is going to be fine. You need to trust Jesus."

"I do. I've been praying and I know he's listening. I believe it's a miracle that Jason didn't break any bones."

Remembering the sick feeling in the pit of her stomach when Jason fell, Meagan had to agree. "He looked so still. I have never been so terrified as I was waiting for him to move."

"I know what you mean. I swear my heart stopped beating when his hold slipped and didn't start again until he opened his eyes." The raw emotion in Adam's voice touched something deep in Meagan. He cared so much for his children.

"You're a wonderful father." The words were out of her mouth before she realized what she had said. She had no desire to retrieve them. He *was* a wonderful father. He was also an incredible man. It would undoubtedly be best to keep that particular opinion to herself, however.

He gave her a look of unadulterated mischief. "Even if I am a regimented stick in the mud?"

She wanted to laugh. "I never said that, at least not in those exact words."

Her raised his brows. "No? I was sure you had said something like that. Or, maybe, yes that's it. More along the lines of running a bootcamp for my children."

Wasn't he ever going to forget that? "I did not precisely say that you ran a bootcamp. I just said that Jason and Mandy's childhood wasn't supposed to be one."

"I feel so much better. Thank you for clarifying."

His laughing sarcasm grated on her nerves. She'd just told him she thought he was a wonderful father. What more could he want? "I came in here for peace and quiet, the operative word being quiet. If there wasn't anything else you wanted to discuss..." She let her words trail off, in hopes he would take the hint and leave. No matter how much she wanted a few stolen moments with Adam, she needed peace more. Her nerves were stretched to the breaking point.

"Actually there are several things I wanted to talk to you about."

Her heart sank. All she wanted was a little time alone to journal and maybe read her Bible. "I'm really not up to a long conversation right now. Can it wait?"

"Don't be a coward."

His words reminded her of their time together in Salem, of how it felt to have his arms around her. She couldn't remember that day without recalling his kiss. She really loved this man. "I'm not a coward. What is it that you want to say?"

He cleared his throat without speaking. Then he stood up and looked out the window. Turning around, he sat back down, this time close enough to take her hand in his. What was going on? Had the stress from Jason's fall done something to Adam's brain?

"I want you to reconsider moving back to the farm permanently."

Somehow, she had not guessed this was coming. It was thinking that he expected her to move back to Scottsdale that did it. Her stomach tightened in knots. Telling Adam no the first time had been more difficult than she could imagine. She didn't know if she had the strength to do it again.

She made a half-hearted attempt to stave off further comment. "We've been through this before."

"I know. But that was before."

The fall. Jason's fall had to be the reason Adam was asking her to stay again. The stress of her leaving had hurt both Jason and Mandy. Adam wanted to protect them, to give them what he thought they needed to be happy. He was convinced it was her.

"Nothing has changed. Not really. I know Jason is confused right now, but he'll remember soon and when he does all of my reasons for refusing to come back before will still be there."

Before Adam had a chance to answer, Mandy came crashing into the room. Her voice rose on an all too familiar tearful wail. "It was all for nothing."

That's it. This time Mandy was going to talk. Meagan fixed the little girl with her best, "You'd better give me a straight answer" glare. "Amanda McCallister, I think it's about time you told me what's had you crying one minute and muttering the next for the last two days."

Tears slipped down the little girl's face. "Jason almost died and it was all for nothing." She pointed an accusing finger at Meagan. "I told him it was a dumb plan, but he wouldn't listen and now you won't come back anyway."

Adam put his hand out and drew his daughter on to his lap. "What plan, Mandy?" His voice was calm, but the tick in his cheek told another story.

Suddenly the child must have realized she had said too much because she stared in horror at her father. "I didn't mean plan. I meant accident."

"Do not ever lie to me, or anyone else, young lady. What plan?" Adam's voice dropped an octave and he enunciated each word with tight precision.

Clearly realizing that she wasn't going to find mercy in her father's current mood, Mandy turned pleading eyes to Meagan. "We didn't mean for Jason to get hurt."

Meagan put her hand on Mandy's knee. She tried to infuse her voice with calm reassurance. "I'm sure you didn't. Would you please explain your plan to your father and me?"

"It was all Jason's idea."

Chapter Thirteen

Adam gently turned his daughter's face until her eyes met his. "I want you to explain this plan from the beginning to the end and I don't care whose idea it was right now."

Mandy swallowed nervously. "All right, Daddy, but can I pray first?"

Meagan watched Adam's body tense and she expected him to deny Mandy's request. "You have five minutes. At the end of that time, I expect you to have your thoughts in order. Understood?"

Mandy nodded, clearly relieved for even a five-minute reprieve. She slid off her father's lap. "I'm going to your study to pray."

"I'll call you in five minutes."

Mandy rushed from the room. Meagan felt intense admiration for the man in front of her. She was desperate to hear Mandy's explanation and doubted very much if she would have willingly given the little girl time alone with God. When she said as much to Adam, he smiled ruefully.

"It wasn't just Mandy I was thinking about. I could use the time to pray and get my anger under control. The last time I went into a confrontation without praying, the children and I lost the best nanny we ever had. I'm not about to risk alienating my daughter."

Unaccountable tears filled Meagan's eyes. She took a deep breath, willing herself to calm down. "You're not going to alienate Mandy."

Adam gave her a self-deprecating smile. "Don't be too sure about that. She and Jason were furious with me when I fired you. She didn't even want me to tuck her in for the first few nights after you left. Jason had his own way of showing his displeasure."

Meagan heard the pain in his voice and longed to comfort him. She felt guilt build up inside of her. His children had withdrawn from him when she left. No wonder he had asked her to come back.

"I'm sorry. I didn't realize." She put her hand out to him, seeking to reassure him. "They love you, Adam. They'll get over my leaving."

He gripped her hand, caressing the back of it with his thumb. The sensation of his touch was so overpowering that she almost didn't hear the words he whispered as his mouth lowered to hers. "I don't think so. I haven't."

Then his lips were covering hers and she couldn't think of anything else but him. The pressure lasted a few brief seconds and then it ended. He drew his head away and smiled into her bemused face. "Will you pray with me before I call Mandy back?"

She could only nod. Adam prayed a few short, but fervent sentences asking for patience and wisdom in dealing with Mandy in the upcoming interview. When he was finished, he and Meagan went to the study to speak with Mandy.

They found her kneeling by the window, talking to God. She looked up when they entered. How composed the six-year-old looked astonished Meagan. Mandy had not just been stalling when she had asked if she could pray before talking to them. Meagan's heart swelled with love for the little girl.

Adam spoke first. "You look ready to talk now. Are you?"

"Yes, Daddy. I'm ready."

"Okay, let's have it. From the beginning." The tension was gone from Adam's voice as well.

"When Mrs. Peer left, Jason and I decided we didn't want another nanny just like her—"

"Mandy, we aren't talking about Mrs. Peer, we're talking about this plan you and Jason came up with for him to fall off the play structure."

"Don't interrupt, Daddy. You said to tell you from the beginning."

Meagan wanted to smile at Mandy's dictatorial manner. She was right. Adam had said to start at the beginning, only he wasn't aware like Meagan was that the beginning started long before she was fired.

"I apologize. I won't interrupt again. Please go on."

Mandy gave her father a skeptical glance, but did as he told her. "Anyway. Mrs. Patty told us that when we really wanted something we should pray for it. She said that God didn't always say yes, but we should pray anyway."

Confusion marred Adam's features, but he kept his mouth sealed.

"Jason and I prayed for a different kind of nanny. We wanted someone to take care of us that liked us and who would let us have fun and not make us sit quiet and put everything away before we were even done playing."

The look of guilt that spread across Adam's face made Meagan's heart constrict. She wanted to tell him it wasn't that bad. That Jason and Mandy had not been miserable—just

203

frustrated. She didn't say anything, however, because she was as anxious as he to hear the rest of the story. She reached out and took his hand. Squeezing it, she tried to convey her feelings without words. He met her eyes briefly and smiled.

"So when the nanny place called and said the new nanny had to go to the hospital, we didn't tell you."

Clearly dazed by his daughter's revelations, Adam just stared at Mandy. "You didn't tell me the Merrick Agency had called?" He shook his head as if to clear it. "No wonder Jason spit his tea out when I mentioned hospitals."

"We were wrong, Daddy. I know that now. But we wanted to help God. We thought if we gave him a chance he could bring us a better nanny." Mandy's voice trembled and Meagan realized that the little girl was near tears.

"Mandy, God doesn't need our help like that. If you have to do something wrong, then you're not really helping God."

"But, Daddy, it brought Miss Meagan."

Adam shook his head. "No. Meagan's car would have broken down in front of our house if you had told me the truth about the nanny. She still would have needed to use our phone and because she has such a generous heart, she would still have offered to watch you two when she found out the new nanny was in the hospital."

Comprehension dawned on Mandy's face. "So we didn't need to hide it from you." Now, she sounded miserable.

"No." Giving his daughter a fierce hug, Adam smoothed her hair. "I forgive you, but please don't ever try to help God by doing something wrong. Deal?"

Mandy nodded her head vigorously. "Deal."

"Now, the rest."

"You're not going to like it. We were trying to help God again."

The expression on Adam's face told Meagan that he already knew he wasn't going to like it. There was no doubt that it had something to do with Jason falling and Meagan was positive she wasn't going to enjoy the telling either.

"It doesn't matter if I like it, squirt. I'm always going to like you. I'm always going to love you. Got it?"

Mandy's little body sagged against her father's legs. "Got it. When you fired Miss Meagan, we thought you messed up all of God's plans. She was perfect and you got mad at her and fired her." The accusation in Mandy's voice drew another guilty frown from her father. "When she stayed gone, we thought we had to do something to make her see that we really needed her."

Meagan felt dizzy. She had suspected, but had not wanted to believe that this plan had been concocted to bring her back. She wanted to cover her ears, certain that the rest of Mandy's words would bring only pain.

"So, Jason had this idea to fall off the barn roof, but I said that was too high. He's just a little boy." The condescending tone in Mandy's voice was almost Meagan's undoing. "It was my idea to go to the park and have him fall there. He was supposed to pretend to get knocked out and then when he woke up he was going to pretend to think that Miss Meagan was Mom."

"Why?" Meagan's voice was hoarse from trying to contain her emotions.

Mandy's gaze shifted to her. "You wouldn't leave if you thought Jason needed you. You love us. We know that."

"And then what? How long was Jason going to pretend to have amnesia?" Adam asked his daughter.

"Until you figured out that Miss Meagan would be a great mom. We don't want a nanny anymore. We want a mom and we think Miss Meagan is perfect."

The words buzzed around in Meagan's brain, tormenting her. *We want a mom and Miss Meagan is perfect.* She lifted her hand to rub her stinging eyes. She felt like she was dreaming. She wanted to be dreaming. Jason had risked injury to keep her at the farm.

Suddenly, Mandy was crying. "But we didn't know he'd really get hurt or have to stay at the hospital. I didn't think you'd get so worried, Daddy or that Miss Meagan would be so scared. Anyway, now it's all ruined." Mandy turned tearful eyes to Meagan. "You know the truth and now you won't stay."

Adam pulled Mandy to him and hugged her. He looked at Meagan over her head. He spoke to his daughter, but didn't break eye contact with Meagan. "Don't worry, squirt. Despite our help, God hasn't abandoned us yet and maybe he'll help Meagan see that she wants to stay because concussion or no, we need her."

He wasn't going to give up and neither were the children. Maybe she was selfish to refuse to take back her job as nanny. After all, it wasn't Adam and the children's fault that she had fallen in love with him. Would it really be that terrible to live in the same house with a man she loved who didn't love her? He had kissed her again. Maybe seeing each other on a daily basis would convince him that he loved her. Regardless, she didn't think she had the strength to say *no* again. Did she have the courage to say *yes*?

Adam insisted on going upstairs to talk to Jason immediately. Meagan and Mandy went with him. Meagan wanted to hear what Jason had to say. A curious sense of unreality had permeated her ever since Mandy had finished her explanation and she felt like she was in the middle of a tornado with no red slippers to find her way home.

&

"I wasn't risking my life, Dad. Stunt men make falls like that all the time." Jason sat propped against pillows on the bottom bed of his bunk. His voice roared in Meagan's brain. *Stunt men did it all the time?* That was his excuse for taking a dive off the high monkey bars?

"You are not a stuntman." Adam's words came out slow and measured. To Meagan's ears it sounded like he was keeping a short rein on his temper. They hadn't prayed before this discussion. The thought flitted across her mind and added to the sense of illusion surrounding her.

Lord, please give Adam patience and peace.

Apparently oblivious to his father's mood, Jason gave a negligent shrug. "I watched a special on it. Don't worry. I practiced falling in the hayloft to get it right." He sounded for all the world like he thought that explained everything.

"You could have broken your neck and been permanently paralyzed." Meagan's voice raised with each word until she was almost yelling.

Jason gave her a wounded look. "I think I did pretty well. I didn't expect to pass out though, but I liked the ambulance ride. It was cool."

Meagan felt hysterical laughter bubble up. She tried desperately to hold it in, but Jason's complacent announcement that he had done pretty well was her undoing. She started to laugh and she kept laughing until tears streamed down her cheeks. Adam and the children were staring at her in concern.

"Dad, I think you better do something. I don't think Meagan's feeling too well."

Jason's words only fueled the hysteria. She wasn't doing too well? The little boy she loved like a son had risked his health, his very life to keep her with him based on a televised special of stuntmen. It was too much to take in.

Adam pulled her into his arms and her laughter turned to sobs. "He-ee could have been k-killed."

"I know, sweetheart, I know." His voice was warm and soothing.

"Don't c-call me sw-sweetheart. I'm not your sweetheart."

"Okay, sweetheart, anything you say."

She pulled away from Adam and tried to look into his eyes. Hers were blurry from tears. "You've got to talk to him. He can't ever do anything like this again."

Adam nodded and rubbed her back. "I'll talk to him."

"Tell him he can't copy what he sees on television. It isn't safe." She hiccuped as another sob overtook her.

When Adam didn't agree fast enough, she grabbed his arms. "Promise me. Explain that stuntmen train years to do what they do. They don't rely on a few falls in the hayloft."

She knew she sounded pitiful, but couldn't make herself care. She had finally hit bottom. She could leave Adam and the children. She could live in a motel filled with prostitutes and drug dealers. She could try to minister to them. But she could not handle Jason risking permanent injury or worse to keep her with him. It was too much.

"Okay, honey, I'll explain."

"Don't call me honey."

"I thought you didn't like sweetheart. You don't like honey either?"

She tried to push away from him. "Don't patronize me, Adam. Can't you tell I'm distressed?"

He smiled at her. "Yes. You need to rest. Why don't you go lie down before dinner?"

Lie down? *Lie down?* Did he honestly believe that a few hours of rest, hiding under the patchwork quilt his grandmother had made, was going to make any difference? She was going crazy and nothing was going to stop her.

Peace.

It was a one-word command and it reverberated through her with the force of an earthquake. *All right, Lord, I'll lie down.*

Adam's softly spoken "Please" was anticlimactic but effective.

"Fine. I'll go lie down. With you and God ganging up on me, who am I to argue?"

He released her and pointed her toward the door. Giving her a small push, he said, "Remember that when we talk later."

She tossed him a disgruntled look and left the room. Like she needed him to remind her that God wanted her to stay on as the children's nanny. If nothing else, that was becoming increasingly obvious.

&

Adam watched Meagan walk out of Jason's room. Her head was bowed and he knew that she was still upset. The deep concern that she had for Jason and Mandy warmed him. He loved her so much. It had taken her refusing to come back to make him realize it. He wanted to follow her and wrap his arms around her, assuring her that everything was going to be fine.

But he couldn't make that promise until he had a certain conversation with his children.

Turning back to Jason and Mandy, he let a parental look of disapproval descend on his face. It wasn't necessary, or even noticed. They were staring in horrified fascination at the door that Meagan had just gone through.

"She was really upset, Dad."

"Yes, she was." There was no reason to soften the truth.

"She could have made herself sick crying, Daddy. Miss Meagan told me that if you cry too much you can make yourself sick. Do you think she's sick?"

Meagan wasn't the only overwrought person in the room. His daughter was headed toward an emotional crisis too. "It's going to be fine. Meagan isn't sick. She's just exhausted and what she needs right now is sleep. As a matter of fact I think you and Jason could both use a nap before dinner as well."

"Daddy! I'm six. I don't take naps anymore." The outrage overrode Mandy's tangled emotions.

"Meagan doesn't take naps either, squirt, but today she's going to and so are you."

"I think that's a good idea." Jason's words did not fool Adam.

"You can both take a nap *after* we've finished talking about your plans to try to help God. Mandy, please sit on the bed next to your brother so I can see you both while we are talking." Mandy obeyed him. Adam reiterated what he had told Mandy in the study about helping God when it required a person to do something wrong. Both children agreed that they would not try to help God in this way again.

"Daddy, aren't you going to talk to Jason about the TV? You promised Miss Meagan."

Adam nodded and Jason groaned.

"Jason, just because you see something on television doesn't make you an authority on it."

His son looked sheepish. "I know. I'm really sorry I scared you and Meagan. It was really scary when I passed out and my head still hurts. I didn't want to say so in front of Miss Meagan because she already looked worried."

Adam understood his son's concern. Meagan had looked like a woman ready to shatter into a million little pieces when Mandy had told them why Jason had taken the fall off of the monkey bars. "I forgive you and I'm sure Meagan does too, but it wouldn't hurt to apologize to her." His son nodded his agreement.

"Now, I want a promise that you will *never* try a stunt like this again. No matter what the provocation."

"I promise." Jason's voice rang with sincerity.

"I promise too, Daddy."

"What about Miss Meagan? Is she going to leave now?" Jason's voice wobbled and Adam knew they had hit the crux of his children's concern.

"I hope not."

"Are you going to ask her to stay?"

Mandy answered Jason's question. "He already did and she said *no.*"

Adam corrected her. "She didn't precisely say no, squirt, she was waffling. Besides I wasn't finished asking."

"I want her for my mom," said Mandy.

Jason nodded and then grabbed his head. "Ow. Me too."

"I wouldn't mind her as my wife either, but I'll have to convince Meagan she wants me for a husband before she can be your mom."

Mandy gave him a calculating look. He shook his finger in her face. "Don't even think about it. I don't need your help. I am old enough to do my own courting. Is that clear?"

Both of his children agreed. Not convinced of their sincerity, he said, "I mean it. If you two interfere in any way, your discipline will be enough to convince you never to do it again."

This time they both gave him solemn promises. "Dad, are you going to discipline us now?" He could tell the thought of a discipline worthy of what they had done had his son worried.

"Actually, buddy, I think a trip to the hospital and all of the guilt you've been feeling is discipline enough. If the sight of Meagan crying uncontrollably isn't enough deterrent not to take a risk like that again, then nothing I can do will be."

"It is. I don't like seeing Miss Meagan cry. I love her."

Mandy agreed with a nod of her head. "I love her too and I don't want Jason hurt again either."

Adam left his children tucked in their beds. He peeked in on Meagan and found her snug under the quilt, but the fan was blowing on high. He stood at the foot of her bed and watched her sleep. *Thank you for sending her to us, Lord. Thank you.*

ॐ

The next morning, Meagan walked through the brush in the forest behind Adam's home. Birds sang in the trees and a warm breeze caressed her cheeks. It was peaceful and peace was what she needed. Adam and the children wanted to know whether or not she was going to stay. She was certain that's what he wanted to talk about this morning. She wasn't ready to talk to him. There were so many thoughts tearing through her mind, clamoring for her attention.

Not the least of which was the kiss Adam had given her when he brought dinner to her room the previous evening. She hadn't wakened from her nap in time to eat with the family, so he brought her tea and a sandwich on a tray. Protesting that she wasn't an invalid had not made any impression on him. He set the tray on her bed, kissed her softly on the temple and ordered her to eat and rest.

Brushing her temple with her fingertips, Meagan imagined that she could still feel the imprint of Adam's lips. She wished she could see into his heart and discern whether or not he had feelings for her. Sometimes, like last night, she was sure he did, but then he would talk to her like a distant acquaintance like he had that morning at breakfast and her assurance would evaporate like the morning mist. He had asked to speak to her later, but his mind had obviously been on other things.

She loved Adam and the children, more than she thought possible. Unfortunately, that was the essence of her problem. She loved Adam. He was everything she could desire in a man. He was loving and loyal. If he loved her, she would never wonder if he were going to betray her the way Brian had.

It was hard to believe she had ever been naïve enough to believe Brian's lies. She blamed the difficulties in their relationship on the stress caused by her infertility. She thought their intimate life had slacked off because it had become too clinical, dependent on her time of month and temperature.

Even after numerous business trips with his secretary, and more late nights at work than she cared to count, she had been taken completely by surprise when Brian asked for the divorce. Maybe she just hadn't seen what she didn't want to see, but then who expects their husband to betray their marriage vows?

She had pleaded with him, not wanting to give up on their marriage so easily. She would never forget the feeling of desolation when he had informed her that his secretary could give him children. He wanted to be a father. He wanted a regular family. She should understand that.

What she understood was that her ex-husband was a cardboard cut-out of a man compared to the character and depth that Adam showed day by day, moment by moment. Adam would do anything for those he loved. That's what scared her. Did he really want to rehire her, or was he doing it just to please his children, against his own better judgment?

When he kissed her, or spoke to her in that warm and sexy voice he seemed to reserve only for her, she was positive he cared for her. If only she could be sure.

The dappled sunlight that fell through the trees warmed her skin. It felt like a hug from God and she reveled in it. If ever she needed His comfort and assurance, it was now.

The problem as she saw it was that if she stayed and Adam didn't love her, it would be sheer pain living in the same house with him and helping him parent his children. If she left, her heart might never heal from losing him and the children. It was a no-win situation, whichever way she looked at it.

She sat down and leaned against an old and weathered tree trunk. Closing her eyes, she sat silent, waiting for the Lord to fill her with His peace about one decision or the other. In her mind she saw an image of Jason falling. Then other images crowded in. Mandy climbing into her lap. Jason squirting her with the mammoth water pistol. Mandy carefully separating the root ball of a tiny seedling to plant it in the flower bed. Jason and Mandy doing their school work. Amidst all of this was Adam. Adam smiling. Adam laughing. Adam arguing. Adam's arms around her. Adam's lips on hers.

She flipped open the Bible she carried, searching for her favorite verses from Psalm 139.

O LORD, you have searched me and you know me. You know when I sit and when I rise; you perceive my thoughts from afar. You discern my going out and my lying down; you are familiar with all my ways. Before a word is on my tongue you know it completely, O LORD. You hem me in—behind and before; you have laid your hand upon me.

Suddenly, she smiled. God had been with her when Brian sued for divorce. He had been with her when she made the move to Adam's farm and he had been with her when she lived in the motel. He hemmed her in behind and before. He wasn't about to abandon her now. If she had the courage to stay with Adam and the children, the Lord would be with her.

Peace settled over her. Her decision wasn't a decision at all. She could no more willingly leave Adam and the children than she would cut off her right arm. Hopping up from the mossy ground, she dusted off her shorts. She picked up her Bible and returned to the house, eager to share her conclusion with Adam. She could see the children helping the farm manager with something near the barn. Adam must be inside the house.

She found him in his study. Before speaking, she took a moment to watch him in his sanctuary. He stared out the window, lost in thought. She thought how this room had seemed imposing when she had first seen it. Now, it felt warm and comfortable. The dark wood looked sturdy and dependable, like Adam.

"Am I interrupting anything?"

He started and turned to meet her gaze. "Not at all. Are you ready to talk now?"

"Uh-huh." More than ready, now that she knew what she wanted to do, she couldn't wait to work out the details.

"Great. Look, why don't we go into the living room and talk this out? I would be more comfortable if we weren't sitting on opposite sides of my desk for this discussion."

His request surprised her. To her way of thinking, his study was the perfect environment for a business discussion. She wasn't about to argue about it, though.

She followed him into the living room. It was wonderfully quiet. She sat on the couch, but Adam didn't join her. Instead, he paced in front of her. If she didn't know better, she would think he was nervous.

"Before we get into our discussion, I wanted to share some news with you. My dean called this morning."

"What did he say?"

He stopped pacing and stood before her. His excitement was palpable. "The dean said that he'd take my request for tenure before the board this month. He seems to think I have a strong chance, especially when they hear about the job offer from Illinois. He doesn't think it matters that I didn't take it. He said the important thing is that I could have and they don't want to lose me."

Meagan jumped off the couch in excitement. She threw her arms around him in a spontaneous hug. "That's great news."

Adam's arms came around her and prevented her from sitting back on the couch. He used that sexy voice, that seemed to be just for her, when he spoke. "It's not a done deal, Meagan."

"But it will be. I just know it."

He winked. "Thanks."

He continued to hold her and her heart started to hammer a rat-a-tat-tat. She wanted nothing more than to mold her lips to his. "You're welcome." Was that husky voice hers? She didn't care. Suddenly, she was tired of waiting to see if he was going to kiss her again. She had told him that she was a grown woman capable of making her own decisions and she was.

Moving her arms around his neck, she pulled his face down toward hers. His lips were warm and inviting when they touched hers. She was immediately lost in a maelstrom of emotion. It felt so wonderful to be in his arms. She pressed her hands into his hair, enjoying the feel of the soft strands against her fingers. She rubbed her body against his and he moaned.

"Meagan."

Like an icy shower, the realization of what she was doing assailed her. She was acting like a wanton. She stiffened immediately, trying to pull away, mortified by her body's movement.

Adam didn't let go. He pulled her closer, sighed and deepened the kiss. He rubbed his hands down her back, letting them rest at the waistband of her shorts. The doorbell rang.

When it rang a second time, Adam pulled away with visible reluctance. "We'll finish this later." His words sounded like a promise.

She shook her head. "No. I don't think we should. We can't keep doing this if I'm going to stay on as your nanny. I don't know what came over me."

"You may not know what came over you, but I think I do. I'd take great pleasure in explaining it to you right now, but that's probably the dean. He said he wanted to come over and talk about the proposal to the board."

Adam gave her another short intense kiss and then pulled away to go answer the door. He came back into the living room with a balding man, easily in his fifties. They were talking like old friends.

"Meagan, I would like you to meet my friend and colleague, Arthur Jensen. Arthur, this is Meagan O'Hare."

The dean gave her a probing glance. She wondered if he could tell that she and Adam had just been kissing. She told herself not to be ridiculous, but that didn't stop a flush from creeping up her cheeks.

"It's nice to meet you, Miss O'Hare." His voice was soft and mellow, but it wasn't friendly. That surprised her. He seemed like he would be a friendly man.

"The pleasure is mine, Mr. Jensen. Would you and Adam care for something to drink?"

"Some of Estelle's ice tea wouldn't be amiss," he said in a slightly warmer tone of voice.

"I'll be right back, then." Adam smiled his thanks as she left the room. She quickly readied the drinks and returned to the living room. She wanted to hear what Dean Jensen had to say about Adam's tenure proposal.

As she came down the hall, she was surprised to hear Adam's raised voice. He sounded angry. She stopped outside the doorway, not sure she should disturb them. "I won't have the university, or anyone else, telling me who to employ in my household."

"Adam, be reasonable. One of the board members' wives saw you together in Salem. She thought you were acting more like lovers than employer and employee."

"So? Is that any business of hers? What I do in my time away from the university is no one's business, but my own."

"In a perfect world. But this isn't a perfect world. Our board of trustees is made up of a conservative lot. If you insist on thumbing your nose at them over this nanny issue, the vote for tenure could go either way."

Meagan was shocked at the dean's words. How could who Adam employed as a nanny have any impact on his bid for tenure? The idea that her staying could jeopardize Adam's chances at tenure twisted her insides into a tight knot.

"I won't have my private life dictated by the university board." Adam's voice was glacial.

"That's part of the problem. You don't have a social life. You don't attend the college functions. A lot of the board members don't know you."

"Arthur, you know how hard it is to attend these functions alone."

"Have you thought about remarrying, Adam? If you had a wife, the board wouldn't care if your nanny was a nineteen-year-old knockout."

"Thanks a lot. As a matter of fact, I am thinking about remarrying, but not before the board's vote and I'm not getting rid of Meagan. My children need her, Arthur."

Meagan stood outside the door, feeling like her heart had turned to lead. Adam was thinking of remarrying. She had no doubt just who he was thinking of marrying either. The children wanted her as their mom, not their nanny. Mandy had made that clear enough. Adam would do anything to give his children a stable and secure family life. Even if it meant marrying a woman he didn't love.

Chapter Fourteen

Something was wrong. From the look on Meagan's face, Adam could guess what it was. She had overheard. He wanted to reassure her that everything was going to be fine, but he couldn't do that in front of Arthur. His dean had already intruded enough on his personal life with his strongly worded encouragement to find another nanny.

Yeah, like he could do that any more than he could tell his lungs to stop breathing or his heart to stop beating. Meagan was going to be a permanent part of his life and it was time that she and everyone else learned to accept it. He had.

There were only two glasses on the tray. Evidently, she wasn't planning on joining them. He smiled and winked at her. She looked back at him with soulful eyes. He almost sent Arthur on his way so that he and Meagan could have their little talk, but she scooted out of the room after placing the ice tea on the coffee table.

She could avoid him for now, but it wasn't going to last.

"Adam, how can you tell me she's just your nanny? You watch the woman like she's your next meal."

"Who said she was just my nanny?"

"So, it is like that. I'll have to say you surprise me. I would never have thought you would expose Jason and Mandy to an affair."

220

Adam stared at the other man. Affair? "What kind of father do you think I am? I'm not having an affair with Meagan."

"But you just said—"

"I'm going to make her my wife."

Arthur's smile could have lit the room if the sun wasn't doing a fine job of it already. "Does she know that?"

"Not yet, but she will."

"You're that sure of her?"

Adam smiled ruefully. "Not really. Meagan has a way of doing and saying the unexpected."

Arthur gave a hearty chuckle. "Well, now this is something I can tell the board. Mrs. Lakely will be thrilled to have discovered the romance first. Why didn't you just say so to begin with?"

Tugging at the collar of his polo, Adam said, "I don't like the idea of the board dictating to me."

"As your friend, I don't mind telling you that you are too stubborn for your own good sometimes."

The doorbell rang. Adam heard Meagan answer it and wanted to groan with frustration when he distinguished Patty and Jake's voices in the hall. Was he ever going to have a moment alone with Meagan?

Patty and Jake walked into the living room and Adam introduced them to Arthur. Jake shook Arthur's hand, before turning to Adam. "We came by to see Jason. How's he doing today?"

"Does he remember about his mom yet?" Patty asked.

"That's a long story." And one he didn't want to go into in front of his dean.

Meagan saved him. "Patty, why don't you and Jake come to the kitchen? I'll tell you all about Jason while Adam finishes his discussion with Dean Jensen."

Arthur stopped them from leaving the room. "Don't leave on my account. I didn't realize your son was sick, Adam. Summer's a rotten time for that."

Adam wanted nothing more than to ask everyone to please leave and come back at a more convenient time, but knew he couldn't do it. Now, he had to explain about Jason to Arthur. "He's not sick. He had a fall from the high monkey bars."

Arthur's eyes widened. "I'm sorry to hear that. He didn't break anything?"

"No."

"Good. Well, I'll be off then." Arthur moved to leave as the doorbell rang once again. This time one of the children came tearing down the stairs to answer it. Adam watched his daughter shoot by the entrance of the living room to reach the front door.

The unfamiliar voice of a man asked for Meagan.

"Oh, no. It can't be."

"What, Meagan? Are you all right?" Adam moved to take Meagan's arm. She was staring at the doorway as if she expected a phantom to walk through it.

Soon, a man and a woman followed Mandy into the living room. The man was tall and had hair the color of a tangerine, sprinkled with gray. His mustache quivered as he searched the room with his eyes. The woman was older, but she bore a striking resemblance to Meagan. Disgruntled, Adam thought there were enough people for a decent-sized party. The woman made a bee-line for Meagan and pulled her into a tight hug. "My baby."

"Mom, what are you doing here?"

"After talking to Patty on the phone the day before yesterday, your father and I decided it was high time we flew up here and found out what was going on. I couldn't believe it when she told me that you'd been living in a motel and your room had been broken in to." Meagan's mother emphasized each word with a pat to her daughter's back.

Meagan glared at Patty, who shrugged her shoulders as if to say, "What did you expect?" Adam felt like glaring himself. All he wanted was a few minutes alone with Meagan and with each chime of the doorbell that desire became more and more far fetched.

"It looks like you've got yourself a house full. I'll see you later."

Adam had almost forgotten the dean was still there. The amusement he heard in Arthur's voice did nothing to improve his temper. "I'll walk you out."

He escaped the crowded living room and led Arthur to the front door. "Let me know if there's anything else you need for my tenure proposal."

"You bet." Arthur looked back toward the room filled with people and the sound of several voices raised at once. "You were right. She's going to keep you guessing. It was time someone jolted you out of your ordered existence."

"Thanks. I'll remember your good wishes the next time I'm approached by another university."

Arthur's smile slipped a little, but he slapped Adam's shoulder. "It's a lot harder to move a wife than children." Adam could hear Arthur's laughter through the closed door.

Taking a deep breath, he re-entered the living room. Meagan's mother had transferred her attention to Mandy. "So, this is the sweet little mite that talked my daughter into moving hundreds of miles away from her loving family."

Meagan rolled her eyes.

Mandy stood shyly, not willing to say anything.

Meagan's father materialized before Adam. "Grady O'Hare." He reached out for a bone-crushing greeting.

Adam surreptitiously shook his hand to restart the blood flow when they were done. "Adam McCallister. It's a pleasure to meet you, sir."

Grady indicated his wife. "And this lovely colleen is Kathryn O'Hare, Meagan's mother."

Adam inclined his head toward Kathryn and smiled. "I'm glad to finally meet you, ma'am."

She didn't return his smile. She gave him a Meagan-glare instead. "Young man, you have a lot of explaining to do."

He hadn't been called young man since he was a freshman in college. It had made him feel intimidated then and had the same effect now. Nothing was going as he'd planned today.

"Mom." Meagan's scandalized voice rose above his frustration.

Kathryn turned to her daughter. "We trusted this man to watch over you and what does he do? He lets you move into a questionable motel. Your room is broken into. You move back into his home, which by the way, has never gone over well with your father. You living with a young unattached man."

Meagan burst into speech, her eyes snapping at someone else for a change. "First of all, Mother, Adam was my employer, not my keeper. Secondly, he didn't *let* me do anything. And third, I'm not living with him. I am living in his house. It is not the same thing. Not. At. All."

Adam wanted to cheer, until Kathryn spoke again. "You said *was*. I definitely heard you say *was*. Are you telling me young lady that you are living in this man's house and you are not in his employ?"

This was too much. Adam had had all he could take. He stepped forward and fastened his fingers around Meagan's wrist and pulled. Meagan's eyes darted to his face. "What?"

He kept pulling as he backed toward the door. "Mr. and Mrs. O'Hare, Jake, Patty. Make yourselves at home. There's more ice tea in the kitchen. Mandy can find Estelle and my housekeeper will undoubtedly provide you with a marvelous lunch, but Meagan and I have some things to discuss. We'll be back in an hour or so." Before Kathryn could interrupt him, he went on. "We'll answer any questions you may have then."

When they reached the front door Meagan asked, "Where are we going?"

"A drive."

She swallowed. "All right."

৪৩

Once they were in the car, Adam seemed disinclined to talk. Meagan didn't like it. The silence made her uncomfortable.

"Did you have to drag me out of the house like a caveman?"

"Yes."

"I can't imagine what my parents thought."

His gaze was fixed straight ahead as he turned the Volvo onto a winding road. "I'm sure we'll hear all about it from your mother when we get back."

She had to laugh. He'd known her mom all of fifteen minutes and he already understood one immutable fact: when she had something to say, she said it.

"You said we had something to discuss." She wanted to get this spurious proposal over with.

"It can wait until we get there."

"Just where is 'there'?"

"You'll see."

"You're starting to get on my nerves."

"Then we're even, because my nerves haven't been the same since the day we met."

She didn't know what to make of that statement. Maybe the strain of the past few days had finally gotten to Adam. "I guess you're wondering if I've decided to stay." She tried to make her voice sound casual, like the decision had been an easy one to make.

He turned his head, briefly meeting her eyes. "Not really."

"Not really? Just what exactly do you mean 'not really'?" Did he think he had her twisted around his little finger and he didn't have to wonder what she'd do because he knew? Well, if he did, he could think again.

"Don't go ballistic on me now, Meagan. Though why I should expect today to be any different from any other day, I don't know." He sounded resigned.

"I am not about to go ballistic, Adam. I merely assumed that since you had asked me to stay on as the children's nanny, you would be interested in knowing my decision."

"I didn't ask you to stay on as the children's nanny."

"I'm not exactly senile. I distinctly remember you asking me this morning if I would be willing to stay."

He didn't answer. Instead, he focused on parking the car. They had been driving for the past several minutes on a logging road up the side of a mountain. Adam pulled the Volvo into an overlook. He got out and walked around to her side and opened the door.

The view was magnificent. A valley of trees swept down from where they stood. Some were saplings, planted to replace the forest that had been cut down. The contrast was startling.

Adam turned to her. "You know this would be a whole lot easier if you weren't trying to glare me out of my shoes." His lopsided grin was almost her undoing.

"It would be easier if you could remember the conversation we had yesterday."

He sighed. "I remember every minute we have spent together. Some of them keep me awake at night."

Did he mean he loved her? She turned and walked away. She needed some distance. Suddenly his arms surrounded her from behind and he turned her body until she faced him. He ducked his head until she was forced to look into his eyes.

"Would you like to know the memories that keep me awake at night?"

She made a half-hearted attempt to twist away, but his voice and his arms were irresistible. She stopped her struggles, wanting to hear what he had to say next. "Yes."

"I remember the look on your face when you soaked me with the garden hose. I remember the way your eyes blazed at me when you thought I wasn't making the right decisions for Jason and Mandy, but most of all, sweetheart, I remember how your lips feel under mine and how your body melts against me when we kiss."

"You do?" Her voice sounded like a mere squeak.

He nodded. "Uh-huh. I do."

She relaxed against him. "If you remember all that, then how come you don't remember asking me to stay?"

"Oh, I remember asking you to stay."

Stiffening in his arms, she tried to pull away again. "Adam. I think I've had about enough of this. First you tell me you didn't ask me to stay and be the children's nanny and now you say you did. Which is it?"

"It's neither. I did ask you to stay, but not as the children's nanny."

She was right. He was going to propose. A battalion of butterflies took up residence in her stomach. "What are you trying to say?"

"I'm trying to ask you to marry me. Say you will. The children need you. I need you."

The children need you. It was like a chant inside her head. Only he had said that he needed her too. Was that because he needed her for the children, or because he needed her for himself?

"I don't know."

Adam's mouth lowered to hers and he spoke with his lips centimeters from her own. "What don't you know? This?" He kissed her softly. "Or this?" Rubbing her back, he pulled her closer and kissed her deeply. Finally, he lifted his lips from hers and released her. "So, what do you say?"

She wanted to believe he loved her, but passion was not love. As much as she adored the children, she could not bear the thought of a loveless marriage to Adam. "I can't, Adam. I wish I could, but I can't." Her voice cracked, but she didn't cry.

He looked shocked. Before his eyes shuttered to hide his expression, she thought she saw pain. "I see." He swung away and stared out over the valley. Abruptly turning back, he said, "No, I don't see. Meagan you melt in my arms when I kiss you. You love my children. Why can't you marry me?"

"It isn't enough for me to be Jason and Mandy's mom. I need more. I need a marriage based on love and mutual respect." There. She had told the truth. She had bared her heart.

"Are you saying you don't love me? The way you respond to my touch says otherwise."

She was tempted to tell him that she didn't love him, but knew that only the truth would answer. "No, that's not what I'm saying. You irritate me beyond belief sometimes, but yes, I love you."

"Well, thank you for that. I love you too, so why can't we get married?"

She felt like the air had been sucked from her lungs. "You love me too?" Didn't the man know that declarations like that were supposed to be made with soft kisses and tender sighs?

She advanced toward him. "You love me too?" She repeated herself in a near shout. When he nodded, looking pleased, but not exactly loverlike, she sighed. "Adam McCallister, I think that's the sorriest declaration of love in history."

She put her hands around his neck and pulled his face down to hers. "I guess it will have to do though," she whispered against his mouth before kissing him senseless.

Adam did not remain impassive in her arms. He pulled her close and responded to her kiss with ardor. Then he showered her face and neck with kiss after kiss while he said over and over again how much he loved her and never wanted to let her go. As he nuzzled her hair near her ear he asked, "Is that better?"

"Much." She sighed in complete contentment against him. "What about your schedules?"

"What about them?"

"I can't promise to order my days like your other nannies did."

"You didn't when you were my nanny. Why should I expect you to be any more cooperative as my wife?"

He was laughing at her, but she didn't mind. He loved her. "Yes. Why should you? But, what about me taking the children to the shelter?"

"Are you saying you're going to want to do that again?"

"I might."

"We'll pray about it."

That sounded reasonable. "Okay."

He smiled. "Anything else?"

"Private school."

His smile dimmed. "We've talked about this."

She snuggled closer. "I know, but now that I'm going to be their mom I can legally homeschool them."

He rubbed her back with a circular motion. She loved the delicious sensations that went clear to her toes. "If you're busy homeschooling, when will you find time to write?"

She had him and she knew it. "I wrote while I taught them before." She nibbled on his neck.

He groaned. "Can we pray about it?"

She spoke against his neck. "Uh-huh."

"Good. Is that all?" He sounded like he was having a difficult time getting the words out. She smiled as she nibbled on his ear before whispering in it. "I snore."

He shuddered. "I'll buy ear plugs."

A grin spread over her face. "I guess that's it." Then she gave herself up to another heart-stopping kiss.

Later, Adam gently disentangled himself from her arms and stepped back. She felt her heart nearly burst as he knelt on one knee before her. "Meagan, I love you so much I can't sleep at night. Will you do me the honor of becoming my wife?" The words were wonderful; the look of love in his eyes was overwhelming.

"Yes, oh yes, Adam. I can't think of anything I want more."

As he stood and pulled her back into his arms, she heard him pray a prayer of thanksgiving. She added her voice to his and they kissed with a reverence and awe for the gift of love that God had given them.

୪

Adam stood next to Jake and waited for his bride to come down the aisle. She had insisted on being married in Scottsdale around her family. He hadn't minded at all. Kathryn and Grady were a force to be reckoned with. Adam had been anxious to meet the rest of their offspring. His gaze scanned the sea of faces and rested on Patty. She smiled with the complacent look of a pleased meddler.

Music filled the outdoor speakers as Mandy, wearing a neon green lace dress, walked toward him tossing flower petals as she went. Her smile was as bright as the sun that shone on their wedding guests. Jason, in a tux with cummerbund that matched his sister's dress, followed behind her carrying a lace pillow with the rings. He struggled to look dignified, but a little-boy grin lurked at the edges of his mouth.

Jason and Mandy had been through the roof with excitement when he and Meagan had shared their happy news with them. The children were already calling her mom and she fit the role like she was born to it. He wasn't surprised. After all, God *had* intervened. Jason and Mandy were thrilled with their new relatives. They had spent the last several days swimming and playing in the Arizona sunshine with their cousins. He was glad they got along so well because Kathryn had offered to watch them while he and Meagan went on a honeymoon.

Next came Meagan's attendants, wearing a rainbow of bright colors. By the time a hush settled over the guests and the bridal march started, he was straining to get even a glimpse of the incredible woman who would shortly be his wife.

When she stepped into view, he almost laughed out loud. Where on earth had she found a lime green wedding dress? That was his Meagan. She smiled at him and for a moment no one else but them existed. Her eyes were misty and his heart responded to the gentle love in them. Grady put his arm out and she took it. Adam's breath caught as Meagan started up the aisle on her father's arm. She was so beautiful. It amazed him that she was truly his. She looked radiantly happy and he prayed that throughout their marriage she would stay that way.

When Jake instructed Meagan's father to place her hand in his, Adam felt the most amazing sense of completeness. He and Meagan were made for each other and he couldn't help once again thanking the Maker of all things. He felt the warmth of tears trickle down his cheeks. Meagan reached out with her glove and tenderly wiped them away. She smiled into his eyes and he missed most of Jake's words on the sanctity of marriage. However, he spoke his vows without hesitation. Meagan's voice trembled and Adam squeezed her hand.

The ceremony was over and he walked Meagan down the aisle amidst cheers and clapping by their friends and family. He leaned forward and whispered into Meagan's ear, "Lime green?"

Her laughter bubbled over. "You didn't expect white?"

"Of course not, my love. Too traditional." His laughter mingled with hers.

About the Author

To learn more about *L.C. Monroe (aka Lucy Monroe),* please visit *www.lucymonroe.com.* Send an email to *L.C.* at lucymonroe@lucymonroe.com. She loves to hear from her readers. You can also join her mailing list by visiting her website.

Look for these titles by
L. C. Monroe

Now Available:

Miss Fixit by L.C Monroe and Nicolette Derens
Annabelle's Courtship (writing as Lucy Monroe)

They walk away from the wreckage of an airplane,
but their hearts and lives will never be the same.

Never the Same
© 2007 Diane Craver

When fashion buyer Kimberly Collins and high school senior Tori Moorhead escape a burning plane, both women make radical decisions that intertwine their lives forever.

Kim's priorities change, especially in the bedroom. She's thankful to be taken to another world—one of love and romance, not of smoke and death. When she decides she wants another child, her husband reveals his own shocking plans for their family.

Pregnant teenager Tori is on her way to get a secret abortion when the plane crashes. The baby's teen father wants to get married. Her dad pushes for adoption. Caught between the two men she loves, Tori struggles to make the right decisions for her baby and the future she dreamed of.

Available now in ebook and print from Samhain Publishing.

Enjoy the following excerpt from Never the Same...

Victoria Moorhead stood in front of her full-length mirror. She looked the same. She placed her hand over her stomach. It felt the same.

But it wasn't the same. Her baby was growing inside her. Why had she and Ryan celebrated their victories so intimately that fateful night? As co-captain of the football team, he was excited when his team won the league championship. Her soccer team had also won their league, so they'd drunk a little too much beer and lost all control.

She glanced in the mirror a last time before climbing into bed. She was wearing the University of North Carolina T-shirt her dad had bought for her on their last campus visit.

"Well, golden girl, you did it," he'd said, using the expression he'd begun to use after the accident that killed her mother and paralyzed him. At first she'd thought he called her that because of her blonde hair. Later, she realized she was his golden girl because the accident had left her uninjured. "God has something special in mind for you," he reminded her often.

Her cell phone rang and she answered it.

"Tori, I can't sleep," Ryan said. "I keep thinking about tomorrow."

She sat on her oversized blue-and-white striped beanbag chair. "I don't think I'll be able to sleep, either. I'm scared."

"Does your dad suspect anything?" Ryan asked.

"No, he thinks I'm going to New York so Blair can help me find a dress for the sweetheart dance." Her half-sister Blair worked for the airlines and she'd booked the flight for her. She felt guilty about lying to her dad, but she couldn't tell him about the baby.

"I don't want you to have an abortion. I've been thinking we can get married. I'll still go to college, and after I graduate and get a job, I'll pay for you to go."

"We're too young to get married now and..." She hesitated because what she'd just said troubled her. How could she be too young to be a wife, but old enough to kill her baby? "I can't lose my scholarship. My dad would be heartbroken. He's lived for the day I go to college and make something of myself."

"I know I'm asking a lot, but please don't go through with it."

"If I stay pregnant, I won't get to go to UNC." Tori sighed. "It's not fair. You won't have to give up anything. Guys never suffer when they get girls pregnant."

"Honey, I'm sorry about everything. I know how much your scholarship means to you. You did get an academic scholarship at Loyola. You could go there and live at home. We could hire a babysitter while you're in class."

"My dad and I always dreamed I'd play on the women's soccer team at the Olympics someday."

"Whatever you do, I love you."

Her eyes teared. "I love you, too."

"I'll drive you to the airport."

"Maybe the plane will crash, and I won't survive. Everything will be out of my hands and I won't have to go through with the abortion."

"Don't say that. Flying to New York is dumb anyhow. Since you're determined to have the abortion, you should just go to a clinic in Chicago."

"I can't take a chance that my dad or anyone learns I'm pregnant." A thought occurred to her. "You didn't tell anyone, did you?"

"I promised you I wouldn't and I didn't. It's been hard not telling my parents, because I think they should know."

"I wish you could tell them, but I'm afraid if they know, they'll try to stop me."

"I'm not sure what they would do."

Weighted down with adult responsibilities, they became quiet. Creating a new life when both of them were kids had been a stupid thing to do.

The only thing left to discuss was when to leave for the airport in the morning. Ryan sounded so sad, Tori was relieved to say good-bye.

After crawling into bed, she held her beige teddy bear next to her chest. She'd slept with this bear for years. Before her mother had died, they'd made a hat and dress out of blue and red material for the bear. The finishing touch was a little heart necklace.

If only she could talk to her mom. What would Mom tell her to do?

She didn't have to think long. Her mother had often told her how thankful she'd been to have Tori. Her mother's physician had told her she might never have a child.

Clutching her bear, she could almost hear her mother's gentle voice saying, Victoria, having you was a miracle. A child is such a precious gift.

She would tell her to have the baby. The realization startled her and she trembled. But her mother was dead and couldn't help. Tori didn't have a choice but to have an abortion.

Maybe after the abortion, God would somehow see to it that her mother could welcome the baby into heaven.

Her tears fell on the bear.

GREAT
cheap
FUN

Discover eBooks!

THE FASTEST WAY TO GET THE HOTTEST NAMES

Get your favorite authors on your favorite reader, long before they're
out in print! Ebooks from Samhain go wherever you go, and work with
whatever you carry—Palm, PDF, Mobi, and more.

samhain
publishing
Ltd

WWW.SAMHAINPUBLISHING.COM